Robert Elms was born in north L
His youth was divided between c   .   schools
and football stadiums. Then he discovered nightclubs.

A graduate of the London School of Economics, he began writing
at *Face* magazine, where he became contributing editor, while
gaining a reputation as style guru and loudmouth throughout the
British media. *In Search of the Crack* is his first novel.

ROBERT ELMS

In Search of the Crack

PENGUIN BOOKS

PENGUIN BOOKS

Published by the Penguin Group
27 Wrights Lane, London w8 5tz, England
Viking Penguin Inc., 40 West 23rd Street, New York, New York 10010, USA
Penguin Books Australia Ltd, Ringwood, Victoria, Australia
Penguin Books Canada Ltd, 2801 John Street, Markham, Ontario, Canada l3r 1b4
Penguin Books (NZ) Ltd, 182–190 Wairau Road, Auckland 10, New Zealand

Penguin Books Ltd, Registered Offices: Harmondsworth, Middlesex, England

First published by Viking 1988
Published in Penguin Books 1989
1 3 5 7 9 10 8 6 4 2

Printed and bound in Great Britain by
Richard Clay Ltd, Bungay, Suffolk

To Albert James Elms

Thank you: S. Adu, L. Barrett, B. Carr
S. Denton, N. Logan, I. Marti

Contents

Prologue

The Prince, a Paddy and the Crack

Our host for the evening was to be the Prince of Bohemia. The Prince, I had been assured, was a hospitable hostelry in Camden Town, where they wouldn't worry unduly about the fact that I am not as yet legally able to place a bet on the dogs or vote for the politician of my choice. I wasn't too worried about getting served; the public houses of N22 had long since stopped bothering me with such technicalities. But there was a certain prickly anticipation taking little baby bites at my guts. And when the first, metallic twang of the approaching southbound sounded, my stomach seemed to jump in some kind of nervous resonance. I looked down at the crease of my trousers and the reassuring shine of my shoes, and strolled a little self-consciously towards the on-coming train. Friday would not be Friday without an edge.

The thing to do when riding the tube is to stand right at the entrance of the tunnel; that way you don't miss anything. You can see the delights on offer in every carriage and still make it up to the driver's end, if need be. Of course if the platform has been good enough to proffer up a treat or two, you just loiter a little, make sure your entertainment gets in first and park yourself accordingly. But on this good night, Wood Green was pretty barren, and I had my hopes pinned on the incoming traffic.

The windrush hit. I saw the driver flash past, clocked a couple of black kiddies and a smattering of good citizens in the first carriage, nothing much in the second, but a pair of definite possibilities in the third. I turned and ran lazily up the platform to where they would land, arriving at exactly the right spot just as the doors opened. I must admit I was grinning to myself with a certain rather vain pleasure as I sat down opposite my prey. I came a very respectable third in the Harringay 400 metres this year.

About fifteen or sixteen, one of them was wearing a white, sleeveless drape dress that was all the vogue. This was definitely her party frock, but well worn none the less. The other, probably the better looking, was in tomboy denim, and was less to my taste. They both had suntans and smelled of soap and a surfeit of cheap products. I hoped they would notice that I was sporting a pair of the finest chinos the Ivy League has to offer, Royals, white socks and a not unfetching ice-blue lamb's-wool – there's no point girl-watching if they don't look back.

But after the customary one stop's worth of ignoring them, in order to firmly establish that I wasn't remotely interested, they went and ruined all my good work by getting up and getting off as soon as we reached Turnpike Lane. I was gutted. I'd figured them to be Leicester Square at least. Life is hard.

So unless new specimens arrived before the Cross, I would have to spend the rest of yet another blue-line tube journey making up little stories about those few members of Joe's public who were going about their boring business in the same carriage. Or else I could play Guess the Destination or Spot the Tourist. Sixteen years spent in the outer reaches of Piccadilly Line land makes a boy good at underground games. Tonight, though, I could always think about tonight, and Astor.

Mickey Astor is going out with Julia Beresford, who is a mate of my sister's; and a man of some standing he is, too. A son of the Cromer Estate, King's Cross, a veteran of the '76 campaign, a fop and an all-round all-right kiddy, Michael Astor found himself driven northwards by his libidinous longings, and there we met. I suppose it was inevitable that we would get on, what with his past and my future, but a stroke of luck none the less.

For, you see, while I am in no way averse to the high life and night-life of north-east London, it does have its limitations. There is fun to be had. Thrills aplenty of a Saturday night on a high road littered with low-life bubbles, sharp schwarzers and squeaky-clean girls of every hue. But I always knew there must be more to life than Elvis impersonators in their brothers' cars and girls who say yes, but don't know why. And now a benign walrus in the shape of one Mr Michael Astor has told me what I've secretly known for quite a while: that the time has come. And the time is tonight, nine o'clock.

In fact, it's only twenty to, and all's not bad. Apart from a wino called Martin, who relieved me of fifty pence by the cunningly simple tactic of telling me honestly that he wanted it to buy a drink, it was a typically uneventful journey. After running up the escalators, stopping only to curse some kind of Swede who insisted on standing on the left, I walked to the ticket-collector, crossed yet another palm with silver, mumbled something about Mornington Crescent and wondered why anybody pays the full fare. Camden Town Station forecourt was awash with all manner of dark and arty gothics, so I figured there must be some dodgy punk band playing at the Ballroom. The air outside felt good.

I wasn't really feeling nervous any more. I did, for a second, have the ludicrous thought that maybe people could somehow see that tonight I was about to become a grown-up big-boy about town for the first true time. It's a bit like those stupid girls who think that having their first bunk-up is going to show, that people will be able to tell just by looking at them that they've been indulging, as if virginity were a facial expression. But still, a boy's first trip to a bona-fide, well-trendy Soho nightclub is no minor landmark in a life.

The Prince, I had been assured, was easy to find – 'up Chalk Farm Road, past the market, second right, and it's on the left' – and so it was. The Prince of Bohemia looked like a pub, all stern and Victorian, green tiled, leaded and frosted and signed, and when I pulled open the heavy wooden door labelled 'Saloon', it smelled just like a pub. Looking round, without looking like I'd never been in before, I saw it was definitely deep in the old style, populated largely by old men sitting at easy-wipe tables on Dralon benches and wooden chairs with varying parts of pints in front of them. The Prince of Bohemia, it must be said, is not a disco.

But there was music playing. Riding nasally high above the dull, almost mechanical, hum of a public house at work was that annoying diddlee folk music so beloved of ageing Paddies mad to sit and sing and sob and fight about that sad old island of theirs. The boy behind the bar, with dark hair that looked like it had been cut with sheep shears and a light-blue bri-nylon shirt with the sleeves rolled uneasily to his forearms, gave me a bright 'Wat'll it be?' as I stood at the heavy carved wooden counter. This was definitely a Paddy pub. I ordered a can of cold lager, so as not to look like one of them, with a burly pint glass, and re-treated to a table for two in one corner of this ill-shaped room full of threadbare people. Still, the Astor would be here soon.

He was a little late, of course, but then that's no more than you'd expect from a man of his stature. I sat down and began to take it all in. There was a couple of middle-aged couples out for the Friday night drink they've had together in here for twenty years. Over by the small, empty stage was a little unlaughing gang of polytechnic people, all fading Oxfam and fading ambitions of Oxbridge, with their over-stuffed roll-ups and empty concern. And then there were the boys. Some of them were fresh over, straight from sites, with the mud of the lump still on their boots and yesterday's pay-packets fast being bartered into beer as they drank away a week's worth of stroppy gaffers and stinging girders.

Then there were the suits: men of varying ages who'd been home between the devil and the deep pint glass. Maybe these were the ones who'd been here longer, with wives and kids to divide their wages between. And back in their council flats and houses in Archway and Holloway they'd scrubbed and pulled on white shirts, ties and uniformly dark suits with shiny arses and knees from overpressing. They all looked uneasy in suits, like children at a wedding. But then, it's Friday, and you've got to make an effort.

And the younger ones, the ones with nowhere else to go, were making an effort to make this a night they'd forget. Already they were singing and laughing, slapping their thighs in time to the constant stream of diddlee music coming from the juke-box in the corner and the constant stream of Guinness coming from the bar. A couple of them were not much older than me. Yet they were sitting there covered in dirt, swapping stories and pints and laughs with the dried-up old fellows with swollen red noses from too long at the bar and hair turned white by too many 'certs' gone down. Where is their self-respect? And, come to that, where is the Astor?

Having ordered a third can of overpriced lager, I wandered over to the juke-box to see if I could do anything about the music. A couple of girlie goths walked out of the toilet, all mascara, fish-nets and northern accents, looking even sillier in this extremely ungothic boozer. I chuckled to myself at the thought that maybe they had taken the name literally and expected to find some dashing Transylvanian rake serving behind the bar. But I guess not.

The juke-box had fading drawings of Jimi Hendrix and the New Seekers on the front and just about everything that Sean and the Sounds, Big Tom and the Mainliners and the Dubliners had ever recorded inside. The ever-growing riot

7

of suits and boots was, I'll give them this, really rocking now. I didn't think they'd notice if I played 'God Save the Queen' and 'The Sash My Father Wore'. But in a section marked 'Sounds of the Sixties', I found 'I Heard It through the Grapevine', slipped in ten pence and strolled back to my seat. It was ten past ten now. Even Mick Astor isn't that fashionable.

'*Bet you wondered how I knew.*' Marvin's voice richer and finer and purer than all the whiskey in their Ireland, came cutting through the rumble of this jaded, heavy old pleasure machine I was sitting in. I was more than a mite confused, even angry, about my absent companion, but enjoying my little cultural triumph, when one of the doddery old suits walking past suddenly stopped.

'Stood you up, has she, son?'

Can you imagine the shame of it? Here was this lumpen old sop of a Paddy suggesting that a girl would do that to me. I blurted out as quickly as I could, 'No, I'm here on my own.'

He grinned a little, put his almost empty pint glass, streaked with Guinness remains, down on the table and sat heavily on the seat reserved for my missing friend.

'Well, you won't mind if I sit down, then?'

What could I do? He was already into his flow.

'I've been looking at you, son, and you don't seem to be having much of a crack here all on your own of a Friday night. So I thought I'd join you. Is that all right?'

The smell of stout and fried food hit me square in the face every time he talked, and his accent was so strong that I had trouble understanding exactly what he was saying. I just sat, not really replying, waiting for him to get it over with and ask me for some money. A few bob would be cheap to get rid of this worn and wearing old embarrassment. I sipped at the last of my lager and muttered something about my being OK, then he smiled gently and said, 'A lager, is it? I hate to see a man without a drink.'

That was a turn-around, him offering to buy me a drink when I already had my hand in my pocket. I thought of making my excuses and leaving, but what if Mick should turn up now? – there was still time. And besides, to be honest, I fancied another drink. I ordered half of lager and watched as he hauled himself out of the chair and walked over to the bar, talking rapidly to all the other old Paddies as he went.

'Hello, there, Timothy, how's the Mrs? Plenty of work on, have you, Brendon? Good. How are you, Tom, having the crack? Been home lately, Sean?' He spoke without waiting for replies, his voice loud enough to hear over the choruses of 'Dublin in the Green' emanating from the most riotous group of building-site rebels over by the bar. He returned quickly to my table with a pint of Guinness, a pint of lager and a whiskey chaser, the three glasses carried with the skill of someone who'd bought a drink or two before. The spirit disappeared before there was time to do any chasing with it, and he swayed a little as he sat back into the chair.

'Are you having the crack now, then, son?'

He was off again, in that indecipherable brogue of his. I looked at him more than a little disdainfully and said, 'What's this crack of yours, then, old man?'

At that, he put his pint down on the round table and began to sing: 'The crack was good in Cricklewood in a pub they call the Crown. There was bottles flying and biddies crying and Paddy going to town . . .'

I butted in, heartily pissed off with his boring beery singing. 'I've had enough of your song, grandad. Just tell me what the crack is.'

His strong, red face, full of broken blood-vessels and the lines of too many years' hard labour, seemed to get suddenly very serious, and he looked right at me with piercing dark eyes for a few seconds before speaking.

'The crack? You're the kind as'll never know it. The English with their three-piece suites and their motor cars and insurance policies will never feel what it's like to sing and cry and laugh with your mates, to tell tales and hear them told long into the night while the drink and the goodness flow. Over in Ireland where 'tis greener than the Wembley turf, where the bishops are all saints and there's never a lizard to be seen, the crack, let me tell you, is mighty. Because we know how to live there, but you starve us and steal from us, until we're forced to come here to work in this grey and godless country of yours, where a man can barely breathe for all the stuffiness, where the young don't talk to the old and the old don't talk at all. Yet despite all that, we keep the spirit alive. And come Friday night, when the work that kills you can finally be forgot, we drink and sing and share in the old ways that you've tried so hard to knock out of us. The crack, little boy. Just look around you and take it in, because you may never see it again; it's a fucking way of life.'

And behind the bar a bell rang.

Part One

A Beano Hunt

Seven of us on platform eight at 6.30. There's a special kind of weary cold that you feel in your bones when you've been up all night. It doesn't matter what it's like outside, you feel cold inside. And right now, after a night of fierce raving that had started to slump about half an hour ago, I was hitting an almost Arctic low, sitting on a sand bucket, wishing Jimmy Kelly would shut up for once.

I'm sure it was Little Anthony's idea that we should get the first train to Bournemouth straight from a night on the town. Then, about half past two, when everyone else was running round the Cucumber Club like lunatics trying to buy some speed for the weekend, he'd opted for the sly pull on a girl from St Martin's, told me he'd see us in the Latin Bar at lunchtime and headed off for a warm bed and a warm body. We'd opted for just a little of the white powder, procured for ten pounds a gram from a character known as Carpet Head, and were suffering for it now.

'I wonder if they'll open the downstairs bar in the Wolf this year?' said Gabriel to no one in particular while strolling purposefully the three yards forwards and backwards between the line and the wall. Only him and Jimmy still seemed capable of speech, and I wondered whether they'd been dabbing their fingers in our collective cache without informing anyone. At that point Paul Diamond came and crouched down next to me.

'Where's it all going to end, Tony?' Paul was smiling and looking puzzled at the same time.

'Alcoholic poisoning, maybe,' I proffered rather weakly.

He continued, without looking up. 'No, I mean we're on a path now. You might not have realized it – most of this mob certainly haven't – but we're making our own rules now. That's quite a responsibility. I just hope we all do it with grace, that's all.'

Here was a nineteen-year-old boy, with a wedge of hair streaked so often he was now a blond in all but name and a tan commenced in Ibiza last August and maintained through the generosity of a girl called Jean, who works in a solarium on the Tower Bridge Road, talking philosophy at me.

'I don't think there's going to be too much grace and poise in our hotel room this weekend,' I said, looking at the bedraggled group of boys waiting for the train.

Diamond glanced up and grinned, the curtain of hair sweeping across his face. 'Oh, they've got dignity all right. I just hope it lasts.' He screwed up his face in a sign of disgust. 'But I'm not mad for an entire weekend spent in a room with them, because I'm not sure if they've got too much hygiene; they're beginning to decay already.' With that he stood up and nodded at the train.

Rolling slowly from whatever siding it had been sleeping in came a Southern Region train that didn't look any fresher than us. Covered in layers of grime and dust, its delightful early seventies easy-wipe livery was largely obscured. But I knew that it meant a respite from the shivering and the dull ache that was climbing up the backs of my legs and into my back. It might even mean a respite from Diamond and ethics. But then, he did have a point.

Various Adidas bags and carrier-bags and Sweeney's tartan duffel bag, which looked like it should have sandwiches made by his mum in it, were gathered up in a hurried, animated silence and we bundled aboard. We looked for all the world like some kind of extremely irregular army off to fight a war that it has little hope of winning. There was even something approaching a uniform, with more than half our number sporting standard-issue Levis and vaguely fifties attire. But when I saw Joe Kelly stuffing shoes and underwear into an exploding Safeway's bag while trying to keep his dinky leather cap in place, I changed my mind. We looked less like a heroic army off to war than a bunch of broken rebels back from defeat. 'The confederacy of the crack,' I said to myself out loud with some pride.

'Shut that bloody door,' said the porter to Jimmy Kelly with some anger.

'We're going to have fun,' said Sweeney.

Just about managing to haul my bag on to the rack above my head, I slumped into the seat next to Joe, put my feet up and began to relax. There weren't too many takers for the 6.40 from Victoria to Bournemouth this Easter bank holiday, and most civilians that were making the journey seemed to have made the decision to avoid our little company. But there wasn't likely to be too many high spirits from this group of children. I was certainly excited about all the anticipated revelry, and I'm sure the rest were too. But for now we were just about all raved out.

Joe was stretched out, silently reading a copy of the *Daily Telegraph* he'd had in his pocket, navvy style, since Leicester Square. I'd stopped questioning him on his choice of reading matter ever since he'd told me his theory about 'understanding thine enemy'. So instead I shut my eyes and waited to drift. I knew the sulphate still running around my body wouldn't let me sleep, but the dark itself was comforting, and I began to sink into the cosy confines of my own solitary thoughts. And my thoughts were of Bournemouth.

Sitting in the Double-O-Egg, with a cardboard burger and a cup of tea in front of me and a nightmare hitch-hike behind me, I'd first met Gabriel and the Kelly brothers. I was only sixteen then, new to the crack, and a mere juvenile at all this lark, with not a clue what to do next. I was down with a mate from school, who bottled out badly and spent his money on the train fare back as soon as the merriment started. I'd heard this was where London went for its bank-holiday beano, so this was where I went too. But what happens? Then suddenly a kid in cropped hair and a biker's jacket was stealing my chips and firing questions about my plans for the weekend and my political affiliations, as if his mouth were an automatic pistol. He told me his name was Joe Kelly, he'd seen my face before in Smith's, the shop he worked in on the King's Road, and if I fancied running with him and his mates for the weekend, I was welcome. Oh, and by the way, did I want to buy a mohair jumper he'd borrowed from the shop that very morning? He was seventeen, he told me later, and intent upon a political career.

From that point on my first Bournemouth had become a blur of names and faces all tumbling into an endless, ever-emptying lager glass: Jimmy Kelly, the languorous *alter ego* to his brother's Artful Dodger, who became a garrulous demon at the mention of drugs; Gabriel, the Don Juan of the tenderloin, a mulatto so sharp you could cut yourself on his razor parting. Then there was Dangerous Jane, the Siren of the Sands, who tempted boys with pints of Snakebite and the warmest heart; Danny Marney, the famed Ealing Escapologist, who could neither read nor write but who told lies with consummate style. He also occasionally told wondrous true tales, fought and swore and stole like a dream and led a crew known as the Holy Children of Row.

And as I got deeper in, I learned the legends of old and the secrets of pleasure. There were the mysterious men who don't see girls. They had a capacity for fun so heightened that they frightened the straight world, while they tempted each other with their collections of the finest fancy socks. There were the girls who did and the girls who didn't, and as time went by, I learned to tell. There were notorieties like Neandersoul Man, the oldest raver of them all, Make-up

Woman, Sean the Boy and Glen the Good, a dealer of repute. There were those who would not give in, and there were dire warnings of groovers who revel in violence and stupidity and must be avoided at all cost lest you get trapped beneath the wheels of their killer Cortinas. And to top it all there were the ancient stories of beds in the sea, orgies in the night and hotels awash with rivers of beer. There was dancing and there was falling over and there was me smiling through it all at seven pounds per night bed and breakfast.

That was how I spent the train journey to this, my third Bournemouth, with thoughts of Bournemouths past. Happy thoughts.

Becoming part of all this had made me happy; so to while away the time I thought about that too. I don't think you really know what kind of people you are like until you meet them. I didn't have a clue who was going to fill the gap where friendship was supposed to be; wasn't even aware most of the time that there was a gap. But suddenly, on finding these boys it was like what did I do, what did I think, what did I want before I met them?

I met them in stages; but I met them all on a hectic merry-go-round within a few weeks of each other; a few weeks after that first Bournemouth, when all these friendships seemed to tumble on top of each other in a glorious scrum. The Kellys were first: Joe exploded on to my dinner plate and into my life with his unrelenting energy. Red-haired, short, with a pink, Paddy glow, he had fine, almost translucent skin, a pair of motor-bike boots from Lewis Leathers in Great Portland Street and a desire to meet the world and argue with it. It seemed to me that he had already succeeded with a large part of it when I was added to his list.

His brother, Jimmy, was a far more simple, steady, though just as appealing prospect. Gentle, straightforward, possessed of a kind of second-generation lyricism, he had the darker, almost mediterranean, tones that some say swept into Ireland with the Armada. He didn't impose himself on life in the way his brother did. But a year older and a good three inches taller (I often wondered whether their mother, Eileen, had been a bit of a lass in her time, they looked so different), he had a definite physical power that showed in his square jaw and his dark, ungiving eyes. He held himself like a man who could handle himself. And, luckily for his loud brother, he could. But he can't really handle drink or drugs. Funny, that.

The Kelly brothers, as people always called them, were the only two male offspring of a rambling, ramshackle Irish family famous throughout the Archway–Kentish Town area for its earth-shattering shebeens. But somehow the two of them had wound up working in the King's Road: Joe in a clothes shop where his wit was the major attraction, Jimmy, unbelievably when you first met him, in a hairdresser's. He was rapidly becoming something of a star stylist, even though he had fingers like pork sausages. He could also draw, he could really draw, and he cut hair just dandy.

The two Kellys were entirely inseparable and they usually completed a trio with one Mr Gabriel Neville McCay, the high-born son of an English woman with a taste for handsome gentlemen in zoot suits. Gabriel was graced not only with true grace, but also with a face that God must have made himself: burnt caramel in colour and full of flowing, angular lines that provided the perfect framework for a pair of dreamy, almond eyes. Gabriel was and is, I believe, the finest-looking man I ever saw, and there were times when I truly believed I almost fancied him. He knew, too. I felt good being with Gabriel because it always seemed as if some of the style might rub off, and you could always catch some of the girls that fell for him. He owned an easy, efficient manner that you couldn't help but like and seemed rarely angry or upset. He modelled but he rarely talked about it. In fact, he rarely talked about anything much, but it never seemed to matter.

But for some reason I seemed to matter to those three, and I must admit I was pretty excited by the fact. I worked hard at first, but why not? Here was something I felt excited by, people I felt excited by. On that same Bournemouth weekend I was introduced to Diamond, but never really got beyond a 'hello'. He was part of a small group of kids from central London, who all looked pretty much standard soulboy stuff; in fact, I thought he might try to sell me a fake Rolex or something. Then someone said he went to Oxford and I was pretty taken aback. I was also a bit jealous.

I met him again a couple of weeks later in Whispers, a chichi Covent Garden cocktail bar where I couldn't afford to buy a beer, and he responded to my greeting by saying, 'They shoot clothes-horses, don't they?' and laughing at my jumble-sale suit. I hated Paul Diamond for at least seven minutes for that. From then on I took to him like I've never taken. He was almost all the things I wanted to be (I've never wanted to be a peroxide blond in silly trousers), and almost always brilliant. And somehow we seemed to start knocking around.

He already knew Joe and Jimmy, and both of them knew MacSweeney, who had not been at Bournemouth because Arsenal still had an outside chance of the League title (they finished fifth and missed Europe). But he was most everywhere else after that. Forever riding in from Hackney, he preached the twin religions of Arsenal FC and militant socialism, which he took almost as seriously as soccer. Mac was a stocky, nondescript kid with acne scars and apparently only one set of clothes, which looked like they came from Marks & Sparks. But he would give you the shirt off his back if you hadn't already told him you thought it was disgusting. He was half-way through a City & Guilds in electrical engineering and as dignified a fellow as you could ever hope to meet. I wish 'salt of the earth' wasn't a cliché.

Little Anthony Costa was certainly a cliché, and a bubble.

A woefully young Greek Cypriot with blue-black hair and a grin wider than Green Lanes, he had a gold chain, a mother who still couldn't speak English after nineteen years here, a brother who owned a kebab house and a clothes collection that was truly immoral for one so young. And, it must be said, he wore it well, ever so well. What is more, I had the dubious distinction of dragging him into the fold after literally bumping into him in Wood Green Shopping City. He was trying to steal a watch at the time, and he cursed me with unrivalled inventiveness for getting in his way. I just laughed and called him a wanker; at which point he took off the overlarge overcoat that he had worn specially for the occasion and offered me out. We've been going out together just about ever since. Come to think of it, I don't think he's been home since. He says that he is going to be a pop star and he makes people laugh. I think I laugh about Little Anthony in my sleep.

There were loads of others, of course, clubs full, and I was still meeting people at a fairly furious rate. But somehow it seemed that these were the people I would be with for life, these young men in a train and a Greek having sex somewhere. Life feels fine. No one really slept.

MacSweeney pulled the sandwiches his mother had made from the bag that looked as if it should have mother-made sandwiches in it, and some people nibbled. Joe did his party piece and produced a couple of cans of beer from his pockets, where you didn't even know that he had pockets, and some people sipped. As for yours truly, I just lay and thought and practised the telling of tales.

Bournemouth for me had been the weekend away that had turned into the way in. Amid all the chaos of a traditional bank-holiday teenage jaunt, I'd made the contacts that were begging to make something of my life. Since that first time just a year ago, I'd changed, become part of something, part of a firm, and now I was back on a firm's outing.

You go away like that because you like it, because there is fun to be had, and fun, we all know, is the finest thing. But also, I knew now, you went away to celebrate.

But I will admit that our little band didn't look exactly celebratory, sprawling out of the station and down the steep hill towards the centre of town. We'd already formulated a dastardly plan of attack. Two of us would book into a hotel and the others would bunk in. Not exactly sophisticated, I'll admit, but tried and trusted. And we trusted that Mad Marrel, the famously insane and unsound owner of the Marrel Hotel would be no wiser than usual.

It was Dave, Sweeney's thin mate who brought up the first salient strategic point as we struggled hotelwards. Looking down at the gaping hole in his jeans, he asked, 'Who looks respectable enough to book the room?'

'Not you for a start, you skinny bastard,' shouted Mac, who likes winding people up, especially his mate Dave.

'Piss off,' came the reply. After all, we had been up all night.

'Tony and me,' said an authoritative voice from the rear of the line. Diamond having spoken there was little else to discuss. Mac and Dave continued their feud for a while, the banter rarely rising above the gutter level of their opening salvoes, while I had a rather aimless conversation about the cut of 'Liberto' jeans with Gabriel who had recently invested in a pair and was now singing them higher than Levis. I felt inclined to defend the old ways. Seventeen and a stickler for tradition.

'All right, then, you and Tony take the stuff and get a room,' said Joe, adopting an officious air. 'We'll sit in the park until you come back with the key.'

So, overburdened with bags, Diamond and I walked up the once impressive, once whitewashed steps of the Marrel Hotel and into the reception. Marrel himself, a tall, bearded man with mad blue eyes and seven children, stood behind the counter like some hirsute, realer than life Basil Fawlty.

'Yes, what do you want?' he said with typical charm, looking suspiciously at the two of us.

Paul spoke. 'We'd like a room, please.'

'A room, you want a room. What do you want to do with it?'

'Stay in it.'

'What? You haven't got a Cortina, have you, didn't come here by car?'

I stammered out an amazed 'What?'

He looked at us as if we were half-wits. 'A Cortina. You haven't driven down here in a Cortina, have you? Or a Capri, come to that. I'm putting my foot down.'

'No, we came by train,' said Paul apologetically, while I tried desperately not to crack up behind him.

'Only I'm not having them any more, not in my hotel, not after last year.'

'Why, what happened last year?' I asked, genuinely curious.

'Never you mind. What sort of room do you want?'

'A twin room with bath, please,' said Paul.

'Hot and cold running girls,' said I.

Marrel twitched in agony at my joke. 'You sure about the car?' His eyes nearly popped out.

Paul Diamond, who'd been a paragon of manners, suddenly seemed to decide that enough was enough. 'Look, we came here by train, we haven't got a car of any kind and we want a room. If you haven't got one, just tell us and we'll go elsewhere.'

Marrel twitched again and stood bolt upright. 'I'm sorry, but you can't be too careful, you know. It goes mad down here bank holidays. You wouldn't believe it – you get all sorts. The room will be eleven pounds fifty each per night. In advance.'

We paid, took the key and began to lug the luggage over to the lift.

'And no pissing in the sink,' he suddenly shouted at our backs.

Within three quarters of an hour all seven of us were safely ensconced in the room, Gabriel was working out seven into twenty-three and Jimmy Kelly was pissing in the sink.

The quieter bits of the First World War must have looked a bit like room twenty-nine that first morning of my third Bournemouth. There were bodies everywhere, sleeping where they could, mumbling and occasionally breaking into mournful song when they couldn't. There were bits of battle kit strewn like debris, half a dozen pairs of loafers, berets and Sam Browne belts, tins of hair spray and shaving foam, Levis in all directions and white socks, white socks as far as the eye could see: fly the regimental colours, boys. I managed to sleep in snatches, not exactly a pleasant sleep, but a necessary one. Dave told me later that he'd had a wank in the toilet. I wished I'd thought of that.

Lunchtime sessions are invariably the best, and, being early in the weekend, all the talk in the mess of a room was of 'advance guards' and 'pre-emptive raids' on bars full of girls to press against and boys to impress. I could tell that they were all just as excited as me. The slang level was rising to meet the occasion; people were polishing shoes and pulling on finer clothes than a twelve o'clock start would normally warrant.

'Borrow us your cowboy boots, Tone.' Joe was standing in his best Browns' shirt, best evil grin and no trousers, looking at me. 'Don't forget that eight quid you owe me from backgammon.'

He said it quicker than I could respond, and I knew he had me beat. I literally couldn't afford to say no.

'All right, but no one else is borrowing nothing else all weekend.'

Everyone nodded in agreement, but we all knew we were

lying. No greater love hath a man than to lay down his labels for his fellow man. And besides, you can only really wear something once.

'Come on, you horrible lot.'

Gabriel was standing to attention and hollering in his best mock sergeant-major voice. He was still playing the army game, but I could sense that people were getting a bit bored.

'Fuck off,' came the almost simultaneous chorus from a couple of Kellys and MacSweeney, who liked swearing. We were now ready to fall out or fall over and play.

As I walked, I watched. There were under-age and over-weight girls with dimpled legs and stiletto heels; little knots of beery boys in blue football shorts and red thighs standing outside the Buccaneer and boasting; men who probably went to Bournemouth every year; old-age pensioners looking grumpy in pac-a-macs and sweet in cardigans; and local boys in heavy-metal T-shirts. It wasn't exactly all human life, but a fair cross-section of the kind of southern English working classes who still make it to the seaside of a bank-holiday weekend.

I can't say I liked them, but I knew them. I'd been dragged to guest-houses as a kid, eaten soggy vegetables and shopped with my mum in British Home Stores. They weren't my people; my people were strolling down the hill beside me talking about possibilities. One of them was singing 'Family Affair' and another was kicking a can in my cowboy boots. The others, those we passed, those I saw, were what I could have been, what you become if you stop thinking. They were what I'd become if I stopped believing.

'Gabby.'

Suddenly my shell of thought was pierced by a south London accent wider than the Walworth Road. A pair of fake Hawaiian wedge-heads were leaping all over Gabriel and ranting rapidly about boozers and boys in the Old Kent Road that I didn't know.

'Right wankers, those two.' Sweeney was standing close to me and talking in a quiet sour voice.

'I don't know them.'

He looked tense and angry. 'You don't want to either; they're right bad news. The one with the dark hair's called Spider, and there isn't a more evil bastard ever walked into Stamford Bridge. He's all pally with Gabriel now, but he's a fucking Nazi. His spar, the humble little one with the disgusting trousers, is overfond of cutting old Asian women for a hobby. Sometimes Gabriel's taste appals me.'

I could see Mac's fists clenching in and out and I figured there must have been some really bad blood between him and the two characters now strolling about fifteen yards in front of us. I don't much care for Chelsea Oberleutnants either, but I hate violence, especially in the mornings. So I did my best to defuse the situation with a spot of diplomacy.

'You're a scabby Arsenal bastard who knows nothing about nothing. Relax and let's get to the pub.'

'I mean it, Tony. If he pushes it, I'm having him.'

'Shut up and let's have a drink instead.'

I knew that the only thing Sweeney liked more than a fight was a drink, and besides, the others, except Gabriel, were already in the bar. So I grabbed Mac's arm and tugged him towards the piece of fallen paradise known to all as the Latin Bar.

Now at this point I feel I ought to describe what it's like in a Bournemouth pub when it's packed raving and the children inside are living like there's not much left of today, let alone the distant possibility of a tomorrow. First of all, though, you've got to get in.

No matter what time you arrive at one of the accredited drinkers in the town, there will be a queue outside. And at the end of the line will be a profoundly stupid brick shithouse in a bow tie, bouncing the door. It's not that the town's publicans are overstrict about fire regulations, but people died in the Black Hole of Calcutta, you know. Once inside the Latin Bar or the Caves, if you did happen to die, they'd dance on your body without waiting for your grave. But there's never really any trouble. Though I guess that depends on how you define trouble.

There's always a boy from Birmingham being sick in the girls' toilets, and just occasionally there's the odd spot of sex and drugs (don't expect any rock'n'roll, though). Then there's the drink. Sure, some of it gets drunk, lots of it gets drunk, but far more of it seems to get spilled or thrown or otherwise deposited on the floor, which after a few minutes is strictly for skaters only. Oh, and yes, it's hot, blisteringly hot and dark, always dark.

Suddenly my daytime became night. We were whisked to the front by a bouncer who owed me a favour, because I'd bought him five beers last year, and straight into the deep end of a dive-bar that was already drowning in the kind of saturated heat that is only produced by human pleasure. It's like being slapped in the face. When you walk into one of those weekend crash courses for the ravers, it physically hits you. This was the first session of the first day, and already there were kids dancing and laughing and drinking and singing and shouting and pulling and buying and borrowing, all to the tune of the heaviest hard-funk backdrop care of Cameo. When you dive in, you either swim with the flow or you get the next train back to bankclerkdom. I think one day I could well swim for England.

I bought Mac the first drink, then he bought me the second, then Paul bought a bit of a round and so did Dave. Then a kid I knew from Islington bought me a brandy that I didn't really want. Then, or at least I think it was then, I got in a heated argument over the current merits of the much-loved Cucumber Club with a Richmond Dull. Then I kind of remember seeing a blonde girl called Tina, who I'd visited once or twice on a lonely night, and I bought her a drink, or maybe she bought me one.

Then I distinctly recall trying to take part in a debate about the merits of the latest Clint Eastwood movie, but I couldn't really find the right words for it because of the heat and the music. So I had another drink and spoilt my chances with a girl I'd long fancied, called Ruth, by spilling a drink down her. Then I definitely had a dance, but then the dance seemed to become a kind of migrant sway in the direction of the toilets. I can really remember that I didn't want to be sick on my jumper and that I would be all right if only I could sit down for a while, or maybe lie down . . .

'Tony, Tony, come on, get up love, before they throw you out, come on Tony.'

Directly above me was hovering the face of an angel, blurred but definitely called Tina and wearing a white vest with the eagle symbol of the GDR on it. I don't know why I noticed that, except her tits were almost in my face as she swayed above me. I felt another swell of vomit beginning in my guts and shut my eyes for a second. I didn't want to be sick in front of a girl, so I took a deep breath before speaking.

'Hello, Tina. Sorry, babe, I felt a bit rough.' Looking round, I could see the place was almost empty, with the debris of a day's debauchery littering the floor. Looking at the girl, she obviously wasn't feeling much better than me and was just about capable of repeating her mantra. 'Come on, Tony, get up.'

It suddenly occurred to me that those so-called mates of mine had left without me and I was stuck with the girl. My mind was clearing pretty rapidly, and I had the horrible thought that we looked like one of the wino couples who do their courting outside King's Cross Station. But then this was no time for aesthetics; I had two people to look after.

'All right, let's get out.'

I hauled myself up from the corner I'd been sleeping in and took the bare arm of the girl, who looked like she was about to take my place.

Sunlight can hit you even harder than darkness, and the fact that it was still daytime came as a stiff shock to an already battered system. It also sobered me right up. We sat down on a low wall in silence, trying to gather some sanity for a second, then she spoke. 'D'you wanna come back to my hotel for a while to sleep it off?'

Well why not? All of my mates had vanished, and I didn't really fancy sleeping with Jimmy's feet anyway. And besides, if I remembered rightly, she'd been all right. 'Yes, why not? Where you staying?'

'Well, it's not exactly a hotel, it's a guest-house and we'll have to get a cab because it's out towards Poole.'

Trust a suburban girl, I thought, but didn't say so. Instead I mumbled a thank-you, kissed her on the cheek and started walking towards the roundabout.

Fifteen minutes later we were pulling up at the end of a nondescript, hedgerowed street of overlarge houses with nameplates and 'Vacancy' signs outside. I wondered if they were describing the inside of my head.

'It's called Beau Regard, and you'll have to go round the back and climb in. Don't worry, it's not too hard.'

'Do what?'

'Well, the landlady doesn't like us bringing boys back, so you'll have to climb in.'

What could I do? I'd come all that way. I didn't exactly fancy a spot of mountaineering, but there wasn't much alternative. She gripped my hand and smiled a would-be lascivious smile.

'Don't worry, it's on the first floor, room number fourteen, third window on the left. I'll leave it open.'

She spoke with the authority of someone who'd done this

sort of thing before. But then, I've always admired spirit in a girl, and I'm no moralist. I just wished I didn't have to work so hard for my pleasures. I went in search of the back.

Confronted with a bleeding great wall, there are two things you can do: go home or look for a foothold. Now I always thought 'because they are there' is reason enough to leave mountains well alone. But I will admit that my hormones were racing a little by now, so I decided a jump was worth the climb. And besides, I'd already spotted a neatly positioned post that would act as a leg up.

One foot on, hands on the top of the fence, push up, one leg on, swing up, and then suddenly I found myself hurtling towards the ground, my knee taking a knock on the way down. I landed with all the grace of a drunken teenager. God, this girl had better be worth it, I thought as I got up, looked down and saw that there was now a fashionable hole in my best jeans. The knee itself was slightly grazed, nothing serious, but I don't like pain at the best of times, and this was not the best of times. Second on the left.

I walked across the bare green garden, saw the open window second on the left and tapped on it quietly. There was no reply so I looked in. I couldn't see Tina, but I could hear water running, so I clambered in, keeping as silent as possible while I navigated a way through the room full of synthetic orange fabric. I quickly saw that the veneered bathroom door was pulled to, but not shut, so I decided to surprise her.

Opening the door as carefully as possible, I saw a girl bent over a quickly filling bath, the cheeks of her bum, white inside the pronounced bikini line, parting just slightly as she played with the taps. At that point I felt a massive wave of nausea hit me again and I guess I let out a gasp.

'Who the fuck are you?' She didn't exactly scream, but kind of turned and shouted and tried to cover up all in one rapid, angular movement. I'm not sure exactly what it was that had made me realize she wasn't Tina, but obviously my realization had made her realize there was somebody in her bathroom.

I just blurted something out: 'Look I'm really sorry, I've just climbed in the wrong room, honest, please believe me.'

I don't know whether it was because my voice sounded desperate enough or because I simply didn't look like a rapist, but she relaxed a little, uncrossed her arms and legs and stood upright, her brown body uncurling to its full, impressive height. I guess I should have left instantly, but I was frozen with shock and embarrassment.

'What the hell are you doing here?'

She was obviously as shocked as me, yet she seemed strangely calm now, despite standing there with nothing on, and I sensed she believed me. I even spotted a hint of a grin at the ridiculousness of the situation and my obvious embarrassment. So without even thinking, I said, 'I am really, really sorry. It was a complete accident. But now I'm here, could I use your shower?'

I really don't know what made me say it. That fraction of a grin, the drink or simply the fact that she was considerably better looking than Tina. And I certainly don't know what made her say, 'You can share my bath.'

I know it sounds like James Bond stuff. But on my life, I'm telling the truth. I think I probably gasped again; you don't really expect long shots to come off. But she just turned and got into the bath and I started to take my shoes and socks off. It's a shit life, I thought, while picking up her toothbrush from the sink. There's certain niceties you should never forget. Especially when you've just been sick.

She was wonderful, but then I wasn't bad either. In the bath it was funny and fun, then warm and soft and fluid, drowning in the water and the flesh so that in the end you couldn't tell one from the other, just a warm, moving blanket of pleasure. Then in bed she took control and rode and steered, dictated and led. She sweated little salty beads of sweat at the base of her spine and the nape of her neck and made me feel very young. I did my best to stay with her, to keep from coming too quickly, to give while she scratched and tensed and finally threw back her hair and laughed. And then we slept.

I knew exactly where I was. It was strange, because as soon as I opened my eyes it all came straight back: Bournemouth, the boys, the bar, the beer, the girl, the wall, the other girl, the bath and the bed that I was lying in. There was none of the looking round or sense of being lost that you normally get after a fierce drink and a foreign bed. Instead I lay there laughing silently at the ludicrous series of events and feeling rather pleased with myself. Of course, I leaned across to see if she really was good-looking. I will admit there was a nasty moment when I thought I might just have lied to myself in my sleep and she would turn out to be a dragon, but I was reassured to see that she was just as I remembered. About five seven, dark hair cut into a short bob, round, rather boyish face (eye colour I couldn't check because they were still sleepy-glued together), and a dark, olive tan that made her look sort of exotic. I noted that she also had a remarkable ability to sleep under scrutiny. What I didn't notice until a couple of minutes later was the time: quarter to nine by the nicely fashionable Braun alarm clock she'd obviously brought with her. There's shocks and there's shocks.

I didn't leap out of bed, I'm too self-possessed for that. I didn't want to wake her, not now. But the pubs had been open for hours, the boys would be missing me, and besides I had a tale to tell. So I got out of bed as gently as possible, picked up the fetid remains of my clothes (putting on yesterday's left-overs is even worse when it's still today) and reached for my pen. I know it's an affectation, but I always carry a black Waterman's fountain-pen wherever I go, just in case. There was a scrap of paper lying on the lovely melamine table provided free of charge with the room. So I began to write a note.

It was only then that I realized I didn't know her name. How do you address somebody that you know carnally but not nominally? I opted for 'lover', and wrote in my finest, practised italic:

Fortune has never smiled so sweetly. I was a wayward mariner in search of a port. You were a paradise island, and I'll never lose the map. We'll meet again.
Tony xxx

I screwed the top of my pen back in place, quietly opened the door and looked back at Sleeping Beauty. She probably won't even get the point of the note, I thought; sometimes my talents are wasted. Then I set about doing my best Colditz impression to get past the commandant of a landlady who was bound to be patrolling her castle.

I've never known whether it's morality or money that makes the keepers of English inns so obsessive about preventing unpaid-for fornication, but it certainly sharpens up your escape skills. Hell hath no fury like a woman who owns a guest-house that you've been bunking in.

Actually, getting out was easy. She was obviously off torturing prisoners in the cellar. Getting into town was harder. There were no cabs, and I was getting short of money anyway. So I walked. It's a long walk.

By the time I got there it was all going off. You can feel fun in the air. It's like bonfire night when you're a kid. Even if you don't see a single rocket or a jumping jack, don't get to eat a sausage or any of the jacket potatoes, you can sense pleasure being had, almost hold it in your hands. Tonight this little seaside town, with its usually sedate air of Victorian, do-it-yourself amusement, was weighed down with the heavy, pungent atmosphere of good times. And it sure was a thrill.

Obviously the motorways and railways of the deep south had been busy transporting the overdressed and underworked of young England down to Dorset while I slept. Because the place was now packed. Every pub, every bar, every street corner seemed to house a splinter group from our insane array of anthropological fodder. And they were all going mad.

From the geriatric hell's angels eating pint glasses outside dingy pubs to baby hedonists lying and buying their way into sophisto discos, everybody was determined to have their own particular brand of party. I figured my party would be encamped deep in the bowels of the aptly named Caves, that being their preferred evening hole. My only problem was a distinct lack of influence on the door. I must admit this was troubling me a little as I approached and saw the hordes of barbarians outside. There's nothing worse than a night spent in the open air with the great unwashed. Rule one in the nightclub bible is NEVER GET BACKED.

But just as I was contemplating a spot of tunnelling, I heard a voice calling my name and saw the world-famous Little Anthony and the Inferiors at the head of the line. My diminutive Greek namesake had obviously made it down on a later train and, along with the Kelly brothers, was just about to secure entrance. I pushed straight to the front, upsetting a couple of understandably irate innocents on the way, put my arm round Anthony, gave him a quick hug and walked with the three of them into the lion's den.

'Where you been?'

'What happened to you?'

'How's it been?'

'You seen Diamond?'

'No, I haven't seen Paul, I've been on a mad one. I'll tell you about it in a minute. It's been a real laugh, Anthony. What happened to you?'

My Greek mate shrugged and spoke. 'Don't ask. I went

all the way to Tottenham with that woman and then got blown out by a sudden attack of the chastities. I couldn't be bothered to argue, so I slept for a couple of hours in an armchair, left and was going to get a train down. But I went into the Co-op to get a sausage roll or something, and as I came out I saw Mick and all that lot from Enfield. They'd hired an open-top Cadillac for the weekend, so I came down with them. Seemed silly not to. A touch of class and all that.'

'You're a jammy bastard, Costa.'

'I know. What happened to you? I hear you had a drink lunchtime. They told me you were probably dead.'

'I nearly was. I threw up and passed out in the Latin Bar, got woken up by that Tina, then went off on this odyssey.'

At that point Joe Kelly came over with three drinks, which was remarkably efficient considering the crush at the bar. He also had Gabriel with him, who was now resplendent in pink suit with Max Beyer back. Now I had a full audience, I could get into telling my tale.

I went through all the details, putting in a few actions for effect. I played up the heroism, played down my embarrassment and, I will admit, I didn't exactly play up the unknown hostess's role in the escapade, except, of course, for making it clear how beautiful she was. But then it was *my* story. It went down well, and despite the predictable derision about my sexual performance, nobody really seemed to doubt that it had actually occurred. Things like that happen in Bournemouth.

Most of the others, it seems, had ended up on the beach, where a massive game of drug-crazed football had ensued. Dave had got thrown in the sea and everybody had laughed. Diamond was missing, presumed pulling a swindle. I'd definitely won the rosette for the day.

We stayed at the bar until the bell tolled, drinking steadily but without the ferocity of lunchtime, which, although no one would admit it, had taken its toll. Then someone evil suggested that we do a little of the sulphate before going on to a club. I actually felt like going home, but didn't want to be branded as a wearer of the pink ribbon, so agreed to rave on. I certainly didn't feel like speeding and I'm not entirely convinced that all of the others did (I'm sure Jimmy already had: he was the keeper of the chemicals and he was awake, which is unusual), but what can you do?

So we trooped off to a nearby public toilet, not the most salubrious of venues, but there you go, and split into two sittings. I was in the first group, crowding into the cubicle with Jimmy, Gabriel and Joe. Jim took the paper envelope out of its hiding-place in his cigarette packet, spooned out a pile of the pinky-white crystals on to the white-tiled ledge and divided it roughly into four small lines. I rolled my remaining ten-pound note into a neat tube and handed it to Jimmy, who quickly snorted his line. It was my turn next, so I bent over, placed the note up my nose, picked what looked like the smallest line and inhaled sharply. The bitter mix of amphetamine and whatever it was cut with bit deep into the back of my nose and made me wince sharply. Here we go again.

Half an hour later and you're running at ninety miles an hour and loving it. Half an hour later and we were in Flanagan's, the black-and-chrome nightmare that passed as a local nightclub, and I was not running or loving. I guess it was a combination of the drink, lack of sleep, lack of food and the fact that something was playing on my mind. But it turned the speed in on me. My brain was racing, but strictly round its own track, making deeper and deeper furrows.

She'd been really nice, good-looking, wonderful in bed and strong, charismatic. I'd really like to see her again, but I was so stupid, leaving like that, that note and all that talking to my mates. What an idiot, how can I get to talk to her again, she'd been really nice, good-looking . . . Round and round it went while I stood alone in the corner of a shitty disco, grinding my teeth in time to the music.

Everyone else seemed to be having a brilliant time. A group of five girls, all with rockabilly quiffs, danced a hilarious formation dance to a specially requested 'Staying Alive'. There was a completely surreal game of bar billiards, using bottles and glasses, the inevitable mooning from a bunch of moron groovers, who were probably from Hertfordshire, and a general air that we were all living in the biblical land of 'soddem all tomorrow'. But not for me. I had a bad touch of the sulphate and soul-ache blues. And then I saw her.

But by that time I wished I hadn't. I was speeding so badly, chewing the inside of my mouth and trying to keep up with a mind that was determined to break all speed records. There was no way I could talk to her properly – I'd just make it worse – but I couldn't avoid her. And I might never see her again otherwise. I was aching so badly; she looked wonderful standing there, even better than I remembered. And then she saw me.

It was a non-committal look, but it certainly wasn't a welcoming one. She was with a small group of people: a couple of boys who looked like art faggots and another girl who reeked of portfolios and pretensions. But my one, she shone way above them, as powerful and calm a beauty as I've ever seen. And here was I, a chattering, chewing wreck. And I had to go and talk to her. I gathered together as much composure as I could muster and walked. My limbs wanted to run and I had to fight to keep them in check in the short stroll round the dancefloor to the back bar where she was standing. I felt terrible, but kept repeating to myself that it would be all right, I looked good and still had the charm. Then it cut like a knife.

'That your piece of pussy galore, then, Tony?' Just as I was about to extend my hand to the fair maiden, Joe Kelly shouted his piece of carefully selected abuse, and I crumbled. She just looked like a stone, polished, cold and hard.

'Been telling tales out of school, have we?'

She couldn't possibly have got the James Bond reference I'd thrown into my story and Kelly had thrown across the room like a dart. But the meaning was pretty obvious. For the second time in our relationship I just stood frozen and speechless.

'I want to talk to you.' I felt totally pathetic, but I didn't know what else to say. She just remained unmoved and said something that I didn't understand at first.

'Come on then, sailor, what have you got to say for yourself?' Her friends laughed knowingly, so she'd obviously been talking too, but I didn't get it. For a moment I just stood looking puzzled, my mind chasing off on its own, and my body badly wanting to follow ... Of course, that silly note. But somehow, because she was taking the piss, I felt a bit better, less guilty.

I looked straight into her eyes, hoped and spoke. 'Let's stop playing games. I want to talk to you and I can't do it in the middle of this madness. Will you come out and walk with me?' Again, I didn't really expect it to come off. Why should she? But I felt better for saying it anyway, less small.

She looked at her friends for a second, then looked at me with her head tilted to one side like she was thinking. 'All right.'

Just two words, but they rocked me back for a moment. Then I realized she was already heading for the door, so I quickly followed. When I got out past the dinner jackets, she was standing in the street, looking stern. I walked up and put my hand on her shoulder. She shrugged it off and began talking in a clipped but slow London accent.

'You were bloody stupid running off like that with just that infantile note and then boasting to all your mates. Bloody stupid.'

'I know.'

'And then you expect to waltz across tonight and pull me like some panting schoolgirl.'

'No, I didn't. I've spent a whole night worrying about you. It was incredibly difficult to walk over to you then, because I was so nervous. I don't expect you to believe me, but I've been plagued by you, felt really sorry, really wanted to see you again, wanted to make up for it.'

'So you should.'

I started to feel a little angry. My blood was pumping like mad. So I blurted it out: 'If you feel like that, why the fuck did you sleep with me in the first place?'

She stopped dead and breathed in, pausing for a second before talking. Only now she sounded totally calm. All the mocking had gone out of her voice and her head was shaking gently as she spoke. 'You amaze me, honestly. You wouldn't ask one of your mates that, would you? I slept with you because I felt like it. I was feeling horny, or hadn't you realized that we do occasionally? You were there and you looked all right. You were lucky, that's all. And then you go and behave like some kind of boy-wonder superstud. You don't know the first thing about women.'

'Teach me.'

She looked amazed. 'Why should I?'

'Because I'm asking you honestly and as nicely as I know how. I'm very sorry for having been stupid, but I like you a lot and I want to get to know you. Please.'

'You don't even know my name.'

Why did she have to say that? That was the killer blow. I just gave up, I couldn't try any more. My head dropped and I turned to walk away.

'Rose.'

I swivelled and looked at her.

'My name's Rose. If you want me, you'll find me. London's a little enough place.'

I couldn't help it, but I broke into a fierce grin. It was like being a reprieved man when you thought they'd already pulled the lever. 'I'll find you. London's my place.'

The rest of Bournemouth went as follows: I got wild and happy, driven happy, dancing happy. I made a fine fool of myself and didn't care, I skipped and I swam in the sea naked, my heart soaring and my genitals shrivelling for all to see. Eventually I crashed out with Mac on the floor of a comrade from Battersea, who had some killer blow that blew my light out. But still, through it all there was a flame burning.

Sunday was quick change and check out, last pennies for lunch at the famed Double-O. Meet up with the firm, including the prodigal Diamond, who, it transpired, had booked himself into the Grand Hotel for two days and two nights with a female sport who had a mole in the middle of her back and a smile that made you melt (or so he said). Together they had thoroughly utilized room and room service, before doing an elaborate runner back down to earth and the Double-O-Egg.

The others, it seems, had played in the sand and then at Marrel's, which had been the place to be. Danny Marney and his wild Ealing Evangelists had somehow stolen the best part of a sound system from a local disco and set up an impromptu shebeen at a pound a head, in the breakfast room. Joe and Anthony had DJ'd, using Gabriel's funk tape and a selection of Russ Conway and Bachelors' albums found in the kitchen. Fun was had, and in the middle of the mayhem a mattress had somehow leapt out of an upstairs window and landed symbolically on the vinyl roof of a Cortina parked below. Don't ask me how that one had got past Marrel.

The man Marrel meanwhile had amazed everybody by producing a bag of blues and proceeding to knock them out at a pound apiece. For his pains he ended up fully clothed in a full bath after the Mad Marney had pronounced his merchandise 'dodgy'. I don't suppose it was.

I'd missed all this, but I didn't mind, for once. I was content to listen, because I'd learned that Fulham had miraculously won away from home and a girl called Rose was studying at the Central College of Art in Holborn, probably in the graphics department. Someone Welsh said Bournemouth wasn't as good as it used to be, but few believed him. No one had any money left. The myth goes on.

On the train home Joe and Mac wound me up mercilessly about being a screaming faggot who liked talking to girls, and then we all talked gently for a while about what friendship meant and how lucky we all were. As we rolled up through the faceless, scarred, waste land of south London, Paul Diamond said. 'Tony, I've got an idea I want to talk to you about when we get back to London, a serious proposition. It's time to change your life a little.'

Fulham Home and Away

'My name is Anthony Martin Ross, I am nineteen years of age, I've got seven O-levels, two A-levels and I'd dearly love a job, but you know how it is.'

I don't like lying, but you know what they're like in the Social. They always find new ways to ask you old questions. And they always expect you to say your 'Hail Marys' about desperately wanting to work before they send you your right and proper. Now, coming from a good Catholic family (when Paolo Rossi got all those goals in the World Cup, I was tempted to reinstate the 'I' grandpappy Ross had dropped when he arrived from Palermo), I've never been over-imbued with the Protestant work ethic. It's not that I'm lazy. The bit about the Os and As is all true – I never missed a day at school and I was good at it. But now I'm working hard, hardly working. I wouldn't take a job if it paid me.

I could have taken a place at college, though, and sometimes when there's nothing on the telly in the afternoon, I think I probably should have done. But I've always hated students, all that fake *angst* and jolly beery japes; it's so petty, so bloody middle-class. It's not a word I like to use, but they never have any style, or any fun and money, come to that. And show me a single one that can dance. I could probably have handled Oxford, all those balls and idiot Sloanes to bait, but I never got the grades and everywhere else seemed second-rate. No, I see myself as more of a Dick Whittington, without all the walking. London Town'll be my fame and fortune, and it's only ever been a tube ride away.

I go through that little monologue with myself once every couple of weeks, on the walk back from signing on. It's such a horrid, nagging, Victorian place that it can get even me down. Not that it worries me morally or anything like that. There's whiskey in my Giro; I sign on strictly for pun money. But they have a way of making you feel grubby that I really resent. Luckily, my name coming so late in the alphabet, I'm on the afternoon shift. I feel terribly sorry for all the Arbuckles and Alis, who have to justify their existence first thing in the morning. I also feel it for the ones who want nothing more than nine to five; the would-be-willing wage-slaves with the empty eyes, who can't even make it on to the chain gang of their choice, because of that woman. But then, as I said, I'm not one of them.

I labour away, like the good modern boy I am, in what I term the 'casual economy'. Not that I supply snide designer-label cashmere to our most colourful casual kiddies, like some less than respectable fellows I know. I'm more in the entertainments industry. And for this fine evening I have to travel for my entertainment.

Fulham Football Club is at home to Bolton Wanderers tonight, and a win will take us out of the relegation zone. The reason that me and my half-wit, elder brother support poor old Fulham, when we live almost equidistant from Highbury and White Hart Lane, is lost in the mists of our particular family mythology. It's something to do with my Uncle Jack on my mother's side, who used to drink with Johnny Haynes and took us to the Cottage when we were mere infants. The reason I continue to go? Well, you do, don't you? And besides, that new black full back, Carter, is a dream. Some things just are.

I always feel robbed reading the *Standard* while riding across London to football. It usually takes up about half of one stop to read twice the four lines about Fulham. And for the rest of the journey it's lies about Ken Livingstone and the latest pop sensation. It is twenty-one stops from Wood Green to Hammersmith, including eleven intersections.

I don't like my brother very much. He's a few of the things I don't like about myself, a lot of the things I don't like about the world and all of the things I don't like about the little world I come from. As a person he's the exact opposite of Dr Who's *Tardis*. Physically he's big, but he's small inside, mean. Three years older than me, yet so emptied of all desire that he's like an old man moaning and shuffling through a life that knows no grace. He also knows no morals and wears brown carpet slippers round the house. But we go to football together. It's all I've got left of what you'd call a family life.

I've got a sister too, who I like a lot. She isn't much to do with me; she's got a job with an insurance company and a kid called Fred that certainly isn't anything to do with me. One of the things I like is that no one knows who it is to do with. I don't think she does. Maria's strong, though; she saves and she reads and she dresses her child in the finest. She thinks and she cares and she knows I care. And one fine day she'll find a way out, not too far, but a step is enough for some. Maria will do anything for you. Well, she will for me anyway.

My mum's all right, kind and good, but she's worked too hard for too long. She's been worn away, like a carpet that's been walked on too often, so that her nerves are a bit too close to the surface. As a result she prays more and more and visits her mum in Peckham. Now that's a bastard of a journey.

My dad's a bastard. Actually, that's not fair. He's funny and well liked in pubs, bloody good-looking for his age; but that's about it. I don't ever remember a day, not one, when he made me feel proud of him, when I wanted to be like my dad. He's always been a man who avoids things, like talking to us and getting angry and sharing. Instead of emotions, he has jokes and excuses. He borrowed a pair of my trousers recently when my brother was in court. I think that's the closest we've ever come to a relationship.

It's not entirely unusual for me to get a little philosophical on the way to football. I've done that walk up the Fulham Palace Road so often, I have to have some distractions. You don't exactly have to dodge the excited throng going to Fulham either. But even without the mass hordes, you can still smell the game, especially at night. Impending football matches have a musty grown-up smell, of overcoats and tobacco, mixed with a hint of onion, and the particular print they use for programmes. You can smell the floodlights too, or taste them or something, because night games always feel so much stronger. At some grounds, of course, you can smell fear, but there's hardly likely to be any terror at the Cottage tonight, unless of course the pies are cold again.

As I walked towards the pub, I finished off our family portrait to myself. Me, I'm thick-skinned, charming, vain and happy. There you have the family Ross, my family. But not my chosen few.

'Hello, Tony.' You get to know people in twelve years of mutual masochism, and there were a fair few familiar faces at the bar to welcome me. 'Your brother's getting them in. Give him a shout.'

I spotted my brother's broad back, with his shapeless dark hair trickling down over the brown suede bomber jacket he's worn every day for the last three years. He was hunched over the bar waving a five-pound note.

I shouted to him. 'Alex, buy us a beer.'

Without turning round he acknowledged me with a desultory wave of his fiver. It was the kind of gesture that might secure you a masterpiece in an auction, but isn't guaranteed to win hearts, especially mine, and he's got some winning to do. And then I spotted the weasel.

A lager arrived along the bar. But my brother retired

instantly to a conspiratorial corner with a character called Billy Smith, who was born to squat Toad Hall. I knew exactly what that meant. Smith cares as much for football as I do for bingo. So Alex was up to his old tricks again.

I stopped thinking about it and had a brief argument with one of the old-timers, who insisted that we hadn't fielded a single decent player since 1962. Now I'm a cynic, but that's taking it a bit far. I also had a chat with Lee, one of the tiny number of Fulham boys who might occasionally have a go, if the odds look favourable. He told me that the Thames Bank Travellers had put up a more than respectable show at Reading the week before. Apparently, it had all gone off in a boozer before the game, and a little mob of Fulham had seen off the cream of the Reading firm. According to my animated source, Tank, our esteemed leader, had performed particular heroics with a wrought-iron bar stool and led the rout. I didn't believe a word of it, but the boasts of hooly boys are always entertaining. I used to run with the herd when I was a child, so I understand the etiquette involved. You never cast doubts on a man's fighting stories. Why spoil someone's pleasure? I don't exactly hold with fighting at football any more, but each to his own, consenting juveniles and all that.

At about a quarter past, just as I was contemplating leaving on my own, Alex bid a greasy farewell to his rodent mate, came over and said a half-hearted 'hello'. We drank up and left for the game in a group of about half a dozen. I intentionally held my brother at the back.

'What are you doing with that wanker, Alex?'

'Billy? He's all right. Besides, what's it fucking got to do with you?' He wasn't angry, just dismissive.

'Nothing, except you're my brother, and I don't want to have to lend Dad my strides again, all right?'

He grinned his horrible oozing grin at my little joke. 'You won't have to lend nothing, and I won't be borrowing any more either.'

I stopped and grabbed the sleeve of his jacket. I almost didn't care as much as I was appearing to. My brother could resurrect the Kray gang if he wanted, and it wouldn't bother me unduly. But somehow I had the feeling that if he could be this stupid then maybe it was in me too. And besides, any man who can love a cause as lost as Fulham FC must have some soul somewhere in him. I was trying to locate Alex's.

I looked hard into his eyes. 'If you get nicked again, you're going down. Think of what that would do to Mum. You've got a shitty job mending broken cars. What more do you want?'

'I want Fulham to do the double.'

Standing outside the Fulham Palace Road end, you could hear a little exaggerated murmur, which meant that the teams were coming out. I turned away from Alex, paid my three pounds to a man in a cap and walked diagonally up the terracing to the spot where we always stood. Scanning the pitch, I saw that Paul Carter, my poetic little hero, wasn't playing. It was just one of those days.

We actually won two–nil. It wasn't what you'd call a great game; it wasn't really what you'd call a good game, but winning does make all the difference. We scored from a rather doubtful penalty half-way through the first half and got a rather charming little goal from Hopkirk after a lovely short passing move ten minutes into the second. After that, the game just about stopped. Fulham seemed shocked to be winning at all; Bolton simply seemed bored. And after a while so was I. The pies were piping, so you couldn't get angry about that, and apart from a tiny, disconsolate group of northerners, huddled dispiritedly together at the open end, there wasn't even anyone to taunt. I felt disturbed.

About fifteen minutes from the end I did something that I never, ever do: I decided to leave early. I'd barely spoken to my brother all game, apart from a perfunctory hug when the penalty went in, and now I was going to travel home alone. I knew I was doing it as a gesture to Alex, and I felt genuinely dramatic as I turned to him.

'I'm going, Alex.'

'All right, I'll see you later.'

'What?'

'I said, I'll see you later.'

Here I was breaking our final bond and he either didn't notice or else he didn't care. I hesitated for a second, hoping he would stop me or something, but he just turned around and continued watching the game. I left.

I must admit, I did stop on the way out to watch Fulham take a corner, but it went straight to the keeper. Other than that, it was straight home with thoughts of grey and blue.

Home is where the programmes are. And my collection of Fulham programmes is stored in the middle bedroom of a former council house, with patio doors and a large back garden, in Wood Green. I share a room with my brother, a house with my family and little else. I don't actually come home all that often any more. Even if I could afford the cab fare back to N22 at three in the morning, I'd still have to convince a cab-driver to take me there. So instead I make do.

But home is still where I call home, still where I read the Sunday papers, kick the cat and keep my clothes. And walking once more up the short garden path, putting my key in the lock and shouting a warning 'hello', I felt like an actor who had played a part too many times. I walked in and straight into the living-room, where a television was flickering its American flicker in the corner. Only my father was sitting watching.

'Did you win?'

'Two–nil.'

'Good game?'

'It was all right.'

He hadn't even looked up yet, and I wasn't sure that he knew which son he was talking to.

'Where's Alex?'

'He didn't come back.'

'Oh.'

'Where's Mum?'

'She's at your nan's.'

Our conversations rarely got beyond one-liners, but usually they had a certain empty wit. Tonight I didn't feel funny. For a long time I'd been quite proud of my background, in many respects I still am. But I'm also feeling more and more constricted, more and more hemmed in by this household and its contents, both those that are human and those that are on HP. The very chair I was sitting in, watching a rerun of *Kojak*, made me feel uncomfortable, with its foul, floral, acrylic cover. So did my father, so I decided to go straight to bed.

Upstairs I took off my clothes and had a look at myself in the full-length mirror on the wardrobe – not bad, could do with a bit more weight perhaps, and a suntan certainly, but still the body of an athlete, even if I hadn't run since leaving school. I put the radio on and instantly switched from Capital, where my brother had left it, to the World Service and got into bed, beginning to calm down.

'Home is where the programmes are.' For some reason the pun I'd invented on the tube home was playing on my mind, and I had a sudden urge to look at my Fulham collection. They were kept in a cardboard box in the cupboard by the window. That battered tallboy, as my mother insisted on calling it, had served as a toy cupboard, hiding-place and wardrobe, for two people growing up and growing apart, for as long as I can remember.

I opened the doors and got sidetracked for a few seconds by an old board game I hadn't played for years, before dragging out the large box full of programmes. Sitting down naked on the floor, I prized open the cardboard lid and looked at the pile. I'd been fastidious as a kid and I knew they'd still be in precise chronological order. I wanted to look at the very earliest issues. Maybe I was trying to re-assure myself with nostalgia, but for whatever reason, I plunged my arm elbow-deep into the box in order to get to the bottom, then my hand hit something hard.

I grasped the angular metal object wrapped in plastic and yanked it up past the pile of programmes. In the split second that it took to wrench the thing out, I had an awful realiz-ation of what it might be.

Standing stark bollock naked in the middle of my bed-room, I was holding a plain white carrier-bag with something heavy in the bottom. For some reason I noticed Alistair Cooke's *Letter from America* had just begun on the radio, and for a second I listened. Then I opened the bag and stared down without breathing. Although I expected it, when you've never seen a gun before, it still takes a while to recognize what you are actually looking at. So I just looked.

Then I felt my guts go and a massive gnawing hole replace them. My fucking stupid brother has gone and got himself a gun and hidden it in my programme box. They seem somehow natural in films, but I've never seen anything more shocking, more terrifying than the small piece of blue-grey machinery sitting in that bag. First I felt sick, then I felt frightened, angry, sad, all the emotions tumbling on top of each other and mixing in a dizzy wave of confusion as I stood staring down.

'Alex . . . Alex.' I don't know why I whispered, don't know why I cared.

Pulling back on the clothes that were lying in a heap by the bed, I knew that I had to talk to my father, to tell him that his first-born had a gun hidden upstairs and was prob-ably planning to use it. I didn't want to take the pistol downstairs, didn't want to touch it, to feel any more dirty.

So I dropped the bag on my bed, where it lay looking sickeningly innocent.

As I walked into the living-room, I could see that my dad had fallen asleep in his chair, the television still blue and twitching.

I shook him. 'Dad, I want to talk to you.'

'What? Sorry.'

'I want to talk to you. It's really important.'

'Not now, Tony. Can't you see I'm knackered?'

'But it's really important, it's about . . .'

'I said, it can wait until the morning. I'll speak to you then. I'm going to bed.' With that he got up and walked towards the door. I thought for a second of standing in front of him and making him listen. But suddenly it didn't seem worth it, he didn't seem worth it. It had all gone.

Instead I put on some shoes and a jacket, checked that I had some money and walked out of the house, up the path, on to the main road, and stopped at the phone-box, where I made two calls. One to Paul Diamond to tell him that we had to make that idea happen, and one to Rose to tell her that I loved her and to ask if I could stay for a couple of days. She said yes. I said, 'I've got to get away.'

Can Pay, Won't Pay

'You can come in, but there's been some trouble.'

Framed by the angular splinters of a once formidable industrial doorway, the young entrepreneurial cadet with the Lenin badge on his cap had a look of resignation on his face. He also had a mix of blood and dirt on his hands and his once white jeans. You should never wear white at a warehouse party, I thought. Especially your own.

'What happened?' said Rose, with a barely concealed grin on her face as she surveyed the obvious signs of carnage.

'A bunch of redneck locals got in early and started taking the piss out of a group of faggots. The boys responded by taking lumps of wood to the locals. Proud of them I was, but I had to send in my bouncer Joe Wyoming to prize them apart. Then one of the idiot yokels made the silly error of calling Joe a "lucozade", which is never wise. So he got a bit angry and it all went off. He accidentally hurt a couple of them, and I'm afraid the décor is not what it was, but it's all right.'

I didn't tell him that he should be young enough to know better. You simply cannot let the animals in with civilized people, mixed dos do not work. But he probably had a gas bill to meet. So I just commiserated with him instead.

As we were talking, a small group of kids walked up the alley clutching xeroxed handouts, looking rather dubiously at the damaged doorway.

'We had an accident bringing the gear in,' said our host with a poker-face and thin eyes. 'It'll be three quid each.'

After a brief conference and a feeble attempt at pleading guest-list, they gave in, shelled out and went in.

'You don't have to pay, of course,' said the warehouseman to me and Rose as we walked past.

'Of course.'

The inner East is fast becoming one of the premier sporting districts of the city. And this was the second night in a row I'd stood in EC1 in the rubble of the industrial waste land turned tenderloin, drinking warm beer.

Mythology has it that the first warehouse party was held way down on the waterfront by a Spanish situationalist group determined to dance capitalism down. It is said that they saw the idea of taking over empty industrial space for shebeens as a potent cultural tactic for post-industrial revolution. Truth is, it was thrown by a rent boy from Glasgow with bad teeth, called Angus. But why spoil the story? Myths are valuable things.

Diamond hadn't done his sums yet, but we (Pleasure Inc.) must have made at least a grand last night out of the continuing saga. And that is ample. Tonight, though, my trip way out east was strictly for pleasure. Well, mainly for pleasure – you must never stop looking.

The labyrinthine grey valley that snakes between the city and the suburbs had once been a zone of much forced labour. Then, as the old world died its painful death, it became a no man's land of scarred space and impromptu doss-houses, where once stood proud banana stores. But now it is being nocturnally reclaimed for parties and shows and suchlike, which is sincerely what I call progress. And so enamoured are we as an organization of this process that we regularly contribute to the renaissance by holding Pleasure Inc. events in the neighbourhood. Of course, in these times of avid interest in the delights of the night, the going is good. And good, I always say, is ample.

Tonight is pretty good too, I thought, as we made our

way through the subverted shell. Not exactly rocking, but a fair crowd, considering. Two well-set-up bars, a half-way decent slide show taking up one wall, and DJ Jay Dee spinning on a raised podium. And DJ Jay Dee is in my opinion the best, no contenders. (He is also on our books.) The theme of this night's extravaganza was 'Fuck the Royal Wedding', which was sprayed in big red letters on another wall. Royal weddings are what they have in Britain when the soap operas sag, and we were on the eve of yet another, which is always an excuse for a bash. And since Joe Wyoming, one-time noble prize-fighter and genuine contender of the parish, had already done a spot of bashing, the atmosphere was surprisingly pleasant.

'What do you think, Rose?' The brothers Kelly had been standing at the bar when we arrived, and the one that does the talking was talking to my girlfriend.

'Not bad. The presentation could have been better; the graphics on the invite are shit.'

Now Miss Rose Cadogan is a graphic designer, so I chuckled. Joe is head of propaganda at Pleasure Inc., so I had a fair idea what he might say.

'Not bad for amateurs, but the crowd is hardly first division. Present company excepted, there's barely a face here. But then, after last night, it's understandable.'

I wasn't going to say anything about generosity. Joe is fiercely proud of what we do, and Rose is just fierce. I thought it was a bloody good attempt and I've always believed that 'the more the merrier' is the truest motto. City night-life is simply the sum of its parts, and the more there is happening, the more will happen. The wider the circle, the more there is travelling round it, including money, money and fun.

It had begun, as most things do, in Soho. Diamond had arranged for us to meet in the upstairs bar of the Blue Posts in Rupert Court. It was just before the night of the short pistol, when my brother's ambitions in life had finally made themselves manifest. But even before that, I knew deep down that a break with the old ways was inevitable.

And there, amid the myriad chatters of a dozen nations, Paul Diamond outlined an idea. We would be rational about it, he said. We would simply do what we were already doing, only more so. He said we would use what we knew, and who we knew, and the fact that we knew how to, to live the life and make it pay, to turn our city and ourselves into the recognized best. We would, he said, start an organization, a company, call it what you will, a company of all the talents.

I made my contribution: 'Doing what?'

'What we will do,' Diamond said, while the Japanese and the Swedes and the Americans sipped at beer that tasted of soap, 'is deal in delight. We will take over the night, organize it, publicize it, and as a result both we and the night will grow rich.' And then, shaking his blond mane in a 'now I mean business' gesture, he leaned forward and said, 'In effect we will do three things.

'We will (1) organize: parties, clubs, fashion shows, concerts, whatever needs organizing.

'We will (2) manage: bands, D Js, acts, anyone who shows promise.

'We will (3) sell: tickets, drink and, above all, pleasure, the ultimate commodity. The only thing we will not sell is our souls. What do you think?'

I thought that just maybe he'd taken too many drugs, but I knew he hadn't, and I knew he was serious. I also knew this was the kind of thing we all hinted at in our more romantic moments. But Diamond is among the least romantic of men. I knew at heart it was a good idea, but also an enormous one. And I wanted to know why he'd chosen to talk to me.

'Because you've got a good mind. That only.'

After a couple of guarded responses he could tell that I was sceptical.

'Look, Tony, we've all been living endless night for the last couple of years. We've all reached "can pay, won't pay" status in London nightclubs, but so what? Where do we go from here? I've finished studying now, Joe's still at that clothes shop, Gabriel's getting by doing bits of modelling, Anthony keeps talking about his band, you D J here and there and work the occasional door; almost everybody is still signing on, for fuck's sake. We're all scrabbling. Yes, you're a face, so you've come a long way from Wood Green, because you can get into discos free. Is that all you want out of life?'

'Pleasure Incorporated.'

He stopped his tirade. 'What did you say?'

'We could call it Pleasure Incorporated.'

He smiled his smile. 'Indeed we could.'

And indeed we did. My hand forced by a boil-in-a-bag Colt 45 and the knowledge that nothing comes to those who refuse to believe, I became a businessman. One year and ten months ago this weekend (don't worry, the plans for the second birthday party are well under way, including using the top floor of Centre Point and a disused underground station by the British Museum), we put on the first event under the Pleasure Inc. banner. We planned hard and long. Diamond assumed his natural role as 'organizer and terrorizer'. I was 'ideas in action'. Joe and Gabby were 'go and get 'em'. Little Anthony and the Barbarian Sex Bastards ('the best band you've never heard,' he assured us) were to be the live entertainment, and Jimmy was the one who knew a geezer with a cash-and-carry in Harlesden that would give us sale or return. For reasons of independence and downright stubbornness, Rose refused to be the 'graphics and design man'. Maybe I shouldn't have called her that.

I'd discovered a massive old disused art-deco swimming-pool in Battersea and convinced the local council into letting us hire it for a 'free-form art event'. (I swear I almost got them to give me a grant.) Diamond organized P A, lights, D J's, trestle-tables and bouncers, and Jimmy actually got the drink together. And as the day drew closer, I arranged some artwork for the tickets, although I admit it was nearly all Rose's ideas.

Armed with our printed pleasure promises, Joe and Gabriel hit every bar and club, clothes shop, hairdresser's and model agency in the Christian world. Little Anthony had a lime-green suit with a pleated back, high-waisted trousers, inverted pleats and jet pockets made specially for the occasion. He also invited us all to a rehearsal of 'the finest, dirtiest, hardest group this side of the Wild Bunch'. And the strange thing was, after two numbers you knew they were. Sex Bastards indeed and Anthony a new star in the firmament.

None of this was too remarkable (except for the fact that Little Anthony could sing), but we'd decided from the off that it would be better to launch Pleasure Incorporated gradually. Better to build up a solid reputation for efficiency and excellence than try an exaggerated extravaganza that could go horribly wrong. But still, we had a few tricks ready for the night.

And when that night came, clubland's telegraphic system was certainly buzzing with the idea that we were going for something far bigger than yet another warehouse party. We intended to be relentless, following up every angle, covering every base and delivering blow after blow. All money would be ploughed back in, all mistakes would be learned from. But first we had to crack 'The Great South London Swimming-Pool Splash'.

Come the good night, Friday, 21 September, after a day of solid hard labour turning the old pool into a suitably seedy waterfront setting, a kind of mock Marseilles, we were ready. There were screens and projections, stripy T-shirts and bell-bottoms and even fake tattoos for all the bar staff and bouncers (that was one of my ideas) and there was nothing else we could do. And then they came streaming into the night.

Word was obviously out and we were in. Hedonist hordes came pouring over the Albert Bridge. Gabriel and Joe had surpassed themselves, proving the worth of big mouths and little lies (free drink, free drugs, free love, even free money had apparently been promised to some). On a fine night when there's little legitimate competition, London can probably muster more than five thousand *aficionados* of the participant sport of the outlaw party. And on this finest of late-summer evenings it looked like they had all brought their little sisters with them.

My arse went. I'll admit it now, but after a week of worrying that no one would turn up, I bottled it badly when I saw them queuing riotously almost into the river and double-parking vertically. Joe and Gabriel, who were manning the door, simply beamed and braced their bouncers.

'There's nothing like turning a few of them away to keep the others happy,' said Gabriel to me as I scuttled to the relative security of the D J booth.

'Sorry, this is a private party,' said Joe.

Even given the 'can pay, won't pay' system, which means that at least the top ten per cent of your punters expect and receive the privilege of free entry due to their status, we were bound to be on a winner. Providing, that is, nothing went wrong. And as the first of the crowd strolled across the floor to the bars and stared in amazement up at the Barbarian Sex Bastards' equipment set up high on the boards (we have to give them some surprises), I couldn't think of a single thing we'd overlooked. I'd already noticed the first of the franchised dealers disappearing into the toilets with a pair of hungry-eyed buyers. What more could they want?

Diamond and MacSweeney, who'd been drafted in to use his City & Guilds in electronics to good effect for once, strolled over slow, like lawmen proudly patrolling their recently pacified domain.

'I think we've done a good job,' said Mac, looking up at the spaghetti of wires running to the equipment on the diving-boards.

'Excellent,' said Diamond.

The hall and the money-boxes were already beginning to fill up, the drink was pouring out as far as the matelots could deliver it, and they were already dancing in the deep end.

'It's going like clockwork,' Diamond said.

And at that point the alarm bells rang.

'Quick, the Old Bill.'

I swear I saw my life, or at least those bits of it that make up my nightmares, flash in front of my eyes. I don't know who shouted. But I suddenly saw half a dozen uniforms strolling through the not exactly uniform crowd. Without speaking, Diamond and I made a dash for the front door. As I ran, I remember praying that the door money was well hidden and trying to calculate just how much we'd be down if they stopped it now. It's a good job I can't add up.

'Who's in charge here?' An officer in a flat cap, flanked by a couple of burly beat boys, was standing in the entrance amid a crowd of overdressed and overtly drunk pleasure-seekers.

'I am.'

It was straight out of *Spartacus*. Me, Paul, Joe, Gabriel and a girl no one knew in stilettos and a leather miniskirt all claimed simultaneous responsibility. Our policeman did not look exactly pleased.

'I am,' said Diamond. 'These are my friends and associates.'

'Well, then, you had better tell me exactly what is going on, sonny.'

Any hopes I might have had for clemency disappeared the minute I saw his manner. Our only remaining chance was Diamond's diplomacy.

'I'm sorry for all this inconvenience, Officer. But can we go somewhere quietly and talk this over?' Paul, his hands behind his back regal style, was the epitome of quiet reason.

'No, we can not. Say what you have to say here, then we can all pack up and go home.'

I could see that even Paul was well worried, but he tried not to show it.

'Look, Officer, I'm terribly sorry about the congestion, but I promise you it won't last much longer. This is a strictly private party, invitation only, for the launch of a new Invisible Arts gallery to be opened on this site. It's all strictly above-board. The council knows all about it.'

Our friendly bobby remained completely unmoved. 'So does every Herbert in London, by the look of it. You've been taking money at the door, there's drink for sale without a licence, and I would guess that you are already well over the fire limit, let alone this lot still out here. Now, if you would like me to order my men to confiscate all the drink and strip-search everybody for drugs, I would be pleased to do so. Let's not argue, eh, sonny? Just be glad you're not nicked.'

I heard the murmur of discontent run through the crowd and the music inside stop abruptly. I was just about to slip out of a side entrance for ever when I saw a sight that will stay with me for the rest of my life.

Somehow, directly behind the back of the policeman, a gleaming, black-and-chrome motor bike – a Norton, I think – with two riders in full black leathers and black, full-face helmets, had made its way through the crowd and was now gliding effortlessly into the entranceway.

The whole crowd, including the Old Bill, stopped and stared as this surreal gatecrasher rolled to a halt right in front of us. There was a massive, powerful silence. The driver remained seated, but removed the helmet slowly to reveal a mane of blonde hair. Everyone let out a gasp of air. It was a girl. Then the pillion, in one of the finest angel leathers I've ever seen, rose and stood in front of the inspector and offered his hand. At the same time he removed his helmet, and as he did so I nearly died. 'We're going to hang,' I thought as I recognized this messenger from hell. For it was none other than Danny Marney, king of the desperadoes, leader of the Children of Row and easily the maddest man in the modern world. Joe Kelly buried his head in his hands and whispered what we were all thinking: 'Oh, no, what's he going to do?'

Marney, helmet under his arm like some kind of latter-day knight errant, whispered something straight into the ear of the Police Chief, and I prepared for a fight to break out. But instead they walked calmly together into the corner. A couple of seconds later they emerged smiling like a pair of old pals. I swear I could have died as the Inspector began to speak, his tone now entirely different.

'Sorry to have troubled you, ladies and gentlemen. Obviously there's been some misunderstanding. I will withdraw my officers immediately and hope that we have not inconvenienced you. If you have any problems, please feel free to phone the local station and I will do all I can to help. Have a good evening.'

And then he was gone.

The music clicked back on, the bars started selling again, the crowds kept coming in and the dealers ran back into the toilets to retrieve the stashes they'd hidden in the systems. Danny Marney turned to talk to the girl still perched majestically on the bike. I had to talk to our saviour, and Paul and Joe obviously had the same idea. I spoke first.

'Cheers, Danny, you saved our lives. But if you don't mind me asking, what the fucking hell did you say to him?'

Without even the merest hint of a smile he said, 'I simply told him it was my party and so he should withdraw his men and apologize.'

Diamond pushed his jaw back up and spoke before me. 'No offence, Danny, but do the Metropolitan Police always do exactly what you tell them?'

'Well, you see, I also told him that if he ever wanted promotion, then it might be politic to let this party continue. Because my father is head of the West London Division of the Metropolitan Police.'

I wasn't the only one who burst out laughing, but I managed to speak as well. 'What, and the idiot believed you?'

At that point Danny got on to the back of the bike, and the blonde girl, who still hadn't said a word, kicked the machine alive. Just as they began to drive slowly into the heart of the party, Danny turned round and smiled. 'Of course he did. It's true.' And with that a single insane cackle cut the air and a motor bike cut the crowd.

The rest of the night, in order not to dwell too deeply on the insanity of the events that had just taken place, I drank far too much and then, I will freely admit, indulged in one half of one hallucinogen. But then, so, it seems, did most everybody. Most everybody, that is, except for Little Anthony, who for the first time in his life was sober after midnight.

When two o'clock, the appointed hour, arrived, the lights were dimmed, the taps were turned and water started to fill the pool. A taped announcement, over the music of a thousand heavenly choirs, filled the air.

'Ladies and gentlemen. Out of the darkness comes light, and into the light steps darkness itself. THE BARBARIAN SEX BASTARDS.'

And when he came on, he came on like Jesus. Like all the

potentates and the pashas and the pimps that ever were; singing the low-down dirty blues in a voice corroded with rust and coated with gold, and indeed we were touched. And when he moved, the girls shook and shimmied and sighed, and the boys all ached and envied and loved. Or so it seemed to me.

And all the time, perched high on the high board, the lime-green suit sending out signals of omnipotence and opulence, we wondered would he fall or would he dive. And throughout the performance he danced on this edge and held us enthralled. And then, as the climax came, the blues became an opera and a tango and a jazz, and he preached perfect, eternal damnation for all those who were deserving. And as he teetered on the very brink, just then, as all around loving fans came in noisy orgasms and it seemed that he must finally become a swallow, it was black and he was gone.

And later I spoke to the star and asked why he hadn't accepted the invitation of the water below. 'Was it the suit?' I asked, trying to fathom his mind.

'No,' he said. 'I cannot swim.'

Little Anthony has long been my friend.

But others swam, and some kissed and one at least fell over, and so our party was voted by all but a few stern killjoys and republicans a true success. This was the beginning of Pleasure Incorporated. And never again did we forget to inform the Metropolitan Police of our intentions and thank them for their attention with a case of Scotch or some such token.

And since that first night we've had many adventures, some few failures, an attorney of our own, with a biblical gait; and a steady rise to a position that could not be called dominance, but certainly prominence.

Through it all our guiding light has been fun, our only constraint dignity. I won't make any wild claims for our group. We've brought about no revolutions, engineered no major changes in the body politic or the thoughts of ordinary men. We haven't advanced architecture, the sciences, the study of the occult or the design of household machinery. We've been singularly unsuccessful at finding a cure for AIDS. But we have been good friends and had good times. And so, through our auspices, have others.

At first, a mere two weeks after our initial fiasco turned fandango, we opened a subterranean den for thieves, cutpurses, inverts, ne'er-do-wells, dope-fiends and record executives, known as Boomtime. Buried deep in the squares of old Bloomsbury, Boomtime was an illegal, after-hours drinking club that specialized in desperate men and wanton women with no desire for sleep. We sold them little, save bad company and tepid beer, and they paid little, but were pleased by the service.

Its steady turnover enabled us to pay for Fran, a talented lesbian photographer, who played fierce chess and manned the door of Boomtime, keeping out undesirables and travelling salesmen and the like. She was a character, and it pleased us all to give her gainful employ. It was also good to have a steady home of our own to meet in after the usual round of nightclubs and parties, for we rarely retired till dawn.

So, most every night, in the remotest corners of Boomtime could be seen various variants of the Pleasure Inc. steering committee, that is, me and Diamond and the brothers Kelly and Gabriel and those of our friends like Little Anthony, and Mac, and Eddie Argento, the Neandersoul Man, and, whenever he liked, Danny Marney. And sometimes Rose came too and I was happy.

As well as the club, which opened its doors for seven glorious months from three o'clock every morning, we also offered regular parties. With a mind to keep always one step ahead, we endeavoured to offer some sting in the tail, such as the time we set up a fun-fair in an old factory, and the carnies mixed with the trendies, and we watched and enjoyed the laughter in the eyes of the punters as they whirled round and round. Another time we became temporarily intellectual and hosted serious lectures on semiotics and Egyptology and marine biology before pumping amyl nitrate through the air-filter system. That was fun.

And so was the night we organized a surprise party for our most irregular customers and took them all pot-holing at Chislehurst Caves. Or the time we held a Nude Rockabilly party in some old Turkish baths, and much salacious sexuality was indulged in by those who cared little for the consequences. Many quiffs drooped that night. And through it all we made ample money and the banner of Pleasure Inc. flew, and sometimes it soared.

We had our competitors, of course. Like Albert, an admittedly charismatic homosexual behemoth, who employed only dwarf transvestites and specialized in masked balls and female wrestling events under the name of the Transsexual Express. Then there were the Furry Dice Men, who made much money and few friends by pandering to the wet-T-shirt tastes of the Cortina crowd. There were, of course, the Clone Twins, with their moustached gay masquerades called Members Only. There was a group called the Red Action Faction Attraction, which regularly threw well-meaning but well-naff political parties; the Western Front, with their parties full of the twat-pack of baby Sloanes; and my personal faves, the Games Room, which promised and indeed delivered acid in every glass of punch.

There were also numerous occasional wastrels and one-off ne'er-do-wells who tried to exploit the night. And it must be said that between us we made the city rock, and the world, and even the media, took notice. And I, it was, who did numerous interviews and the like. My mum and Aunty Dolly, who follows my career avidly, particularly liked the picture in the *Sunday Times* colour supplement.

On the other, quieter side of our set-up we dealt with the outside world. After a while we learned how to sell tickets to music and cultural and sporting events to those members of the general public who were anxious to see the entertainments on offer. Rarely did we do our own jobbing out there on the streets, for we subcontracted the finest spivs and scalpers to ply their trade under our expert guidance and with our now considerable resources. And in this way we developed the holy of holies: collateral.

And then there was our asset, our star. Paul Diamond, with his flair for management and his way of talking in incomprehensible but impressive riddles, decided that he would make our Little Anthony into a major force on the swinging music scene; and so he did. He played their silly record-company games with one hand tied behind his back and invented new ones with the other. He wound them up and tied them down. He beguiled them and bruised them, teaching and touching them. And even though he despised them for their expense accounts and tour jackets, he always treated them to the utmost in politeness and manners. Even when he discovered that they all had homes in Hertfordshire.

To pull off the deal we promoted a few, very few, very special Sex Bastards' appearances. These were always secret and private and unannounced, and, of course, everybody knew and talked about them. And as a result Little Anthony and his Bastards became, for a while, like ghosts haunting the boardrooms of all the various major record companies, who slavered for his signature. And then one day, after many Japanese lunches and much enjoyable debate and speculation, our attorney with the religious gait nodded his august nod, and signatures were delivered and an advance obtained.

Pleasure Incorporated now had its first major recording artist. Little Anthony had a suit in gun-metal-blue gabardine with Italian-cut trousers and cloth-covered buttons, made specially for the occasion.

We also took on board a brace of record-players of the highest repute, two of the finest photographers in all of London Town, a distinguished video whiz-kid and, I must admit, for a short time, an artist who had paintbrushes but little talent. And so we were agents. And all the time money came in and we went out, and we worked out equitable and amicable ways to divide the wedge among ourselves, so that none was unhappy and all could have fun. Sometimes it all seemed a little too much like work. Yet other times I would boast that I had never worked a day in all my life.

Occasionally, I will accept, I got carried away on the aristo ethic and expected to be recognized in bars and restaurants and the like. But not too often. For, after all, I had little real money as of yet, and I still lived in Kilburn with Rose. But I had a lifestyle and now and then a life of style, and was, all in all, respected. Though, it must be said, hated by some. But then, I quite liked that too.

And I quite liked this party this night before the royal wedding. I had a dance with Rose, who was looking oh, so fine, aware that many eyes were on her. And I had a good drink, a civilized, cool drink, and lots of talk of football and also baseball with boys who really knew and loved their sport. So when Diamond appeared with Anthony and suggested that we should adjourn to Soho because he had something to show us, I was not entirely of a mind to go.

'What do you want us to see at four in the morning?' I asked.

'Shut up and get in the car,' he said.

Seven of us – four from Pleasure, Anthony, Rose and Jimmy's girlfriend, Kaitlin – squeezed into Joe's old Citroën, its hydraulic suspension struggling to lift us off the ground, and headed west. Paul, who had the unmistakable air of a man who is thoroughly pleased with himself, refused to tell anyone what it was about. But he kept dropping typically cryptic hints about the Chrysler Building and a place in the sun. It takes about fifteen minutes to drive from Old Street to Soho when the only traffic is a few cautious drunks.

Soho, when the raincoats and haircuts have all gone home, is a static, melancholy place. It always reminds me of a tired old whore who's done her work for the night, but can't sleep, so she sits up and drinks, silently, slowly alone. Soho at deep night is languorous and blue. Those who are still up move without haste knowing that tomorrow they must rush again. And as we parked the car in Soho Square and began to walk south, we moved in a respectful, almost silent, procession, through the warren we knew so well. I manoeuvred myself next to Paul and spoke quietly.

'Come on, Diamond, where are we going?'

'Meard Street,' he answered, without looking at me.

'What, is it a party or something?'

'Not yet.'

I've always hated mysteries and I was beginning to get a bit irritated. The others, though, seemed happy enough, chatting quietly and floating down Dean Street, past the Italian restaurants and the Snooker Club. Paul suddenly swung an extravagant right as we hit Meard Street. That avenue-cum-alleyway, with its row of old Georgian houses, its gay disco, shoemakers and Chinese salmonella shop, has long been one of my favourites. It has always had the best selection of streetwalkers in the tenderloin, and now that we were walking down it, I was anxious to know what for.

About thirty yards up the street, in front of a long-decrepit Dickensian whores' den, with cracked windows and net curtains, called The Golden Girl Club, our glorious leader suddenly stopped. With his back to the building and his face to us, he cleared his throat in a theatrical manner and began to speechify.

'Boys and girls, friends and associates of Pleasure Incorporated, I would like to begin by apologizing for the absence of our dear comrade Gabriel. Sadly, he could not be with us on this most auspicious occasion as he is off bunking somewhere . . .'

At this point a tramp, who'd been snoozing in Dean Street, walked round the corner to see what the commotion was and stood next to me with his hands buried deep in his tattered raincoat pockets.

'The date today is July 22nd, which, I must inform you, is something of an anniversary. It is precisely two years to the day since Tony and I first met round the corner in the Blue Posts and decided to embark upon the little enterprise which has led us here. And it has led us here because of this . . .' Here Diamond plunged way down into his rarely violated pockets and produced a rather anonymous pair of keys, which he dangled teasingly.

'This, children, this magnificent little edifice, long known to one and all as the lowest, least sanitary, cat-house in all of the Soho Klondike, is all set to become the home, headquarters and hidey-hole for the above-mentioned entertainments corporation. Downstairs will be the Pleasuredome, new haunt for the discerning *cognoscenti*, upstairs the nerve-centre and occasional doss-house for Pleasure Incorporated. Us . . .'

At this point the tramp standing next to me broke into spontaneous and enthusiastic applause. Diamond bowed and opened the battered door.

'Ladies and gentlemen, welcome to our Chrysler Building, our place in the sun.'

As we walked into the decaying old building, with its angled wooden floors and peeling-wallpaper walls, the details were explained to an excited crowd by one extremely loquacious Mr Diamond in a far less flamboyant manner. The five of us had put down fifteen grand, almost all of the sum total of Pleasure Inc.'s ready capital, on a dirt-cheap 47-year lease and were taking out a mortgage to meet the rest and transform the place into a 'self-financing posh HQ'. All the figures had, of course, been checked with the feared attorney, and he'd given a sanguine go-ahead. We could just about afford it, but, more importantly, we could no longer afford not to. This meant no more business calls from Gabriel's mum's spare room in Finsbury.

As Paul explained all this, he led us up the battered stairway through a series of dark and dirty old rooms that smelled vaguely of stale sex. Having inspected the neglected upper parts, we returned downstairs, me holding Rose's hand hard and beaming like the boy who got the Scalextric set. I felt tender and very in love with all the people present (save for Kaitlin, who always got up my nose, and the tramp who followed us in), and when Diamond switched on the light in the torn red-velvet reception of the former Golden Girl Club to reveal half a dozen bottles of champagne, it felt like the perfect day. All this, and Fulham had just sacked their idiot manager.

Paul did the business with the first bottle (yes, the tramp got some) and made a toast 'to Pleasure'. Then he went over to the corner and switched on a box that had been sitting there, and grinned as the familiar bass line hit first: '*These are our good times*', went the song. And so they were.

The Singing Girl and the Holiday Inn and Other Stories

One evening in a nightclub in which I had little interest, I met a woman with a strong arm and a beguiling smile, who drank Australian beer from a blue can and told me a story. Truth be told, I think the story was about her, and it was the story of the singing girl and the Holiday Inn. It went like this.

Born with a good face to a good family, the girl managed for a while to overcome these setbacks and bruise her shins and shout the odds with the best of them. But there came a time when all their little pressures multiplied, when they spoke to her in serious futures and small amounts. They said she must work hard and look neat. She was a smart girl, she could go far. They said she could marry well and before that enjoy a career, maybe even in computers.

This girl, who in her silent moments could spar with the greats and run like the wind, was full of secret longings. But because she was never given to believe, in time she shrank to fit their clothes. In truth she came from a very poor family indeed, because they were scared to the marrow. Despite all their Capodimonte and having a new car every three years, they were terrified of music and dissension, modern art, foreigners, ambition and nuclear war. And in the end they wore this girl – their girl – down until she was frightened too. And so she forgot that she could sing.

So as she grew older, the girl moved along a straight path, and perfection played little part in her life. But deep down, recalled only at odd moments, such as when travelling up escalators or crossing Waterloo Bridge, she knew that she had a capacity for fine things. After all, as a child she had loved trains with dark-green livery, running-boards and polished brass number-plates. So surely that proved something?

But rare memories aside, she played their game, and because she was good, she played it well. Her parents had her framed picture on their mantelpiece and they were duly proud. But she never once sang for them or anybody else.

Instead she worked hard and was successful, leaving school well qualified (though, she admits now, badly educated), and despite all the recessions and depressions of the time, she walked without trying into a good job. There she met a series of good men, but perplexed her parents rather by settling down with none of them. Instead she buckled down to her work, hid her beauty and love of green livery and at length was rewarded by being sent on a course to test her management potential.

This course, to be held in Birmingham, was to be attended by all of the most promising junior-grade employees in the whole of the British Division of the Multi-national Corporation. They stressed that it was important, but that it would also be fun. Deep down she doubted everything they said, especially the part about fun.

But Birmingham – she had never been there. She was to stay at a Holiday Inn; she had been told they were beautiful and sophisticated, all conveniences and all luxuries. 'A thing to strive for and enjoy,' her parents said. 'A rare treat,' others said.

Riding up on the train, with its Formica tables and its foam-rubber chairs, made her melancholy, because it reminded her of just how beautiful her old green trains had been. Then, when she walked out of New Street Station and saw that Birmingham was not a city at all but a motorway service station, she sank even lower. Still, the hotel would bring elegance and style.

So imagine her sadness when, instead of plush and charm and style, she was presented with a cardboard computer key to a room full of Teasmades and televisions and artificial fabrics everywhere, including on the bed. Her spirits drained away. She dropped her bag on to the acrylic orange bed-cover with green flowers on it, hung her clothes in the melamine wardrobe, switched on Radio Two and washed her hands with the tiny bar of soap that she removed from its plastic wrapping. Even the electric shock she got from the patterned, plastic carpet when she called the lift was just accepted with resignation. This is the way of the world, she thought.

But by the end of the day, after she had endured the endless, mindless, corporate drivel of her course and the endless, artless advances of young executives in ill-fitting grey suits and ill-conceived grey shoes, she felt tired and angry. Refusing all the offers of prawn cocktail and steak and salad, she returned alone and lonely to her room. Such was her depression that, when faced once more with all this ugliness and acrylic and air-conditioning, she thought first of crying and second of suicide. But rather than jump from the double-glazed windows or sit in a warm bath and open her veins, she resolved to act.

The first thing to go was the bedspread; simply removed and placed outside the front door. This was followed by the pillowcases, the Teasmade with its powdered milk, the picture of a horse in a meadow, the shower cap (real people get their hair wet, she decided), the sachet of shampoo, the foam bath and the orange-covered seat, the embossed note-pads and writing-paper, the logoed pen, all the plastic cards and instructions, the Gideon Bible, the brochure about Birmingham and the one about the myriad joys of Holiday Inns. The curtains, instead of being jettisoned, were reversed and painstakingly rehung because of their plain white lining, which she thought just fine. And all the while she worked at dismantling their dream environment, she hummed an aria that she had not heard for years.

She did think about unscrewing all the foul, round, plastic handles from all the drawers and cupboards. But by now she was tired and happy and ready for sleep. So she hung out the 'Do Not Disturb' sign and slept.

Next day (she was disturbed, of course), the second day of a five-day course, she was happy and stroppy and found herself making jokes at the expense of all the grey shoes and singing snatches of *Carmen*. And when the day was over, she returned to the hotel, armed with her own choice of shampoo and bath oil, a plain white cotton towel and an old framed photograph of a matador that she had picked up from a junk shop in her lunch-hour.

She was disappointed but hardly surprised to find that they had restored her room to its former tawdry glory. Instead of becoming despondent, she simply repeated the process, singing out loud and lustily all the while. And in a moment of real joy she hung the photograph (she later discovered that it was of Litri) on their nail and sat and looked at it in all its awful beauty.

For four days she waged this undeclared civil war, each day discarding and rehanging and singing all the while, gaining in strength with each engagement. By the fourth day she was taking the battle to the enemy, reversing pictures in corridors, hiding paper umbrellas and plastic straws in the cocktail bar when it was closed and writing the truth on menus. All the little Englanders on the course suspected that she was unwell. For she sang and argued and questioned and generally behaved in a manner unbecoming to a potential junior executive.

And on the last day of the course, with the knowledge that her card must by now be severely marked, she bought a bottle of tequila and some salt and lemon from a local well-stocked shop. Making no excuses, she avoided the farewell party to be held in one of the function rooms of the Holiday Inn and retired to her room, intending to drink while she dismantled.

Imagine her surprise upon opening the door to find that they had left her room exactly as she had left it, reversed curtains and all. For a second she didn't know how to react – they'd taken away her war, and a certain sadness overcame her, for she had never thought of winning. But then it dawned on her that winning was exactly what she'd done. And winning, she now knew, felt very sweet indeed.

So in a gently celebratory fashion she opened her bottle of tequila and her salt and her lemon and took a drink in the old style. Then she went into the bathroom and collected her toiletries, took her clothes from the melamine wardrobe (somehow the fake veneer didn't seem to matter any more), placed them neatly in her case and finally removed her matador from his place on the wall. She didn't sing while she did this, thinking that maybe she should save her voice.

At the front desk she settled her affairs with politeness and charm and inquired after the time of the next train to London. Twenty minutes later she was sitting behind a large newspaper, staring at the scenery and smiling because the 'Situations Vacant' column would soon be one job larger.

The thing that's wrong with computers, she thought, is that they cannot sing. Because, of course, she could, and knew now that she would.

In the same year as I was told that story, two other events occurred that must be recounted here. The first concerns my brother, Alex.

When I left home that night, what was, and certainly seems like, years ago, my family was a bad taste in my mouth that had to be spat out, severely rinsed. I kept contact, maybe going to see my mum once a month, phoning occasionally. But I didn't want to have to keep explaining myself and I couldn't explain them.

When we met it was like we were in a family encounter parlour, separated by a thick pane of glass so that there was no physical contact, no pain, no pleasure, nothing approaching honesty. My mum adored Rose, but I would never let them get too close, almost as a punishment. I wasn't ashamed of my past. The working-class bit has always been worn like a badge, but somehow I didn't want it weaving into my future. My sister could still squeeze my arm and call me a fool but everybody else and everything else was at one remove. And, to tell the truth, I didn't much mind.

I'd long desired to escape, and it seemed churlish to moan about missing the mailbags. So you do lose little things, but they were being replaced by the delights and the dangers of the real world. Then Alex went and shot an old man in the City.

It was a Thursday evening – I know because Prince had just been on *Top of the Pops* and I'd spent a while musing on bell-bottoms – when the phone rang.

'Tony, it's Maria.'

It's not that I didn't recognize her, but she hadn't rung in nearly two years, so I was bound to be a bit taken aback.

'*Maria*, your sister, you fool.'

'Oh, sorry, Maria, I didn't get it for a minute. What's the matter? Fred all right?'

Her voice was calm as ever. 'Yes, he's fine, looks a bit like you, poor sod. No, it's the one with a younger mental age than Fred. Alex has finally fulfilled his promise in life and gone and done it.'

I was still completely confused.

'Done what?'

Now her voice was a mix of concern and comedy. 'He was trying to pull some stunt or other, I don't really know the details, but it seems, believe it or not, to concern a shipment of toilet-rolls. Anyway, it all went horribly wrong and somehow Alex fired the gun he just happened to be holding into the leg of a 72-year-old porter. Thankfully, he's all right and he certainly isn't going to die, but Mum just might, so you'd better come over.'

I was amazed at the girl. That was our first real conversation in years, and I realized instantly how very great she was. 'I'll be right over.'

Rose volunteered to come with me, but I knew I had to go on my own; I couldn't hide behind her. So I drove through the crosstown traffic of an early evening thinking about what had happened. The bit about Alex had seemed so inevitable for so long that I wasn't remotely surprised. But somehow I saw him in a different light tonight. I've never really known anyone sadder than Alex. You can't really blame him. He's never had free will because he's never known the joy that makes for possibilities. Alex has lived all his life in half-lights, because that is all he can see. Prison won't really be any different; it's all shades of grey to him.

But I did feel for my mum, and even my dad, who must be seeing so much of himself in Alex right now. And Maria – what a brilliant person. If only she could find a way forward.

As I drove too quickly north by north-east, I felt, for the first time in a long time, part of that family. Made me shake a little. I've never really felt grown-up before. Walking into my own house, for the first time I didn't feel like the naughty boy who'd managed to run away from home for a while. I had to help my mum, not hide things from her. For the first time too I wasn't frightened that N22 was going to pull me back again. I was just pleased that I thought I could maybe help.

I'm sure that you can feel tears in the air, that they add to the humidity level. The house was wet with tears that night.

My mum looked small and old and exhausted. She'd spent all day inside police stations clutching a rosary, and it showed. My dad wasn't handsome any more, just red-faced and wiped out. I wanted to tell them that Alex wasn't worth all this pain. He can't feel pain himself.

But instead I told them I'd do everything I could to sort it out, handle the legal side, see that Alex was OK. For once I wasn't doing something for them to prove that I could, to prove my independence, but because I wanted to, because I loved them and knew that I was part of them.

Maria was a marvel, holding it all down, ringing aunts and uncles to tell them that they'd probably be getting a shock in their morning papers and staying wonderfully calm. She even managed to have a laugh with me about it all in the kitchen, and I began to realize that I had missed out on her for so long because she didn't fit my prejudices. She didn't wear the right colours.

And over the next few weeks, as the whole silly, sorry drama of Alex and the great bog-paper robbery uncurled, I began to grow really close to my sister. My mum and dad were all right too. They were a bit lost in this world, but that's all. They were pleased that I was prepared to play such a part, and I was pleased that they were pleased. I didn't really give a shit about Alex, although I never said that to them or him. But I did about them, and it felt good.

Alex's story, as it unwound in Crown Court, was a complete parody of errors; like all the bungled Ealing robberies that never really were. My brother and two other great criminal minds of our age were in cahoots with a Mr Big in the glamorous world of international toilet-roll trading. He tipped them off about an underguarded shipment of shit-sheets, and they were supposed to intercept and redirect it to a warehouse in Shadwell.

Of course, it all went laughably wrong. They got the timing totally fucked up and ended up trying to pull the whole thing off in the middle of Fleet Street in the rush-hour. There's never been a more accurately reported hijack in the history of disorganized crime. They only had to look out of their windows. And what they saw was a juggernaut-load of loo-roll rolling round the street, and not a Labrador puppy in sight. Instead there was my brother up to his ankles in it, turning round and round and finally shooting the doorman from the *Express* building through the back of his leg with a sawn-off shotgun.

Alex said in court that the gun had gone off totally by accident, and I, for one, certainly believed him – he's never done anything by design in his entire life. He also pleaded guilty. I thought he should have pleaded insanity. Who could have argued? But instead he got a wallet-full of press clippings to keep him warm in his old age and a six-year sentence for armed robbery. I was surprised they didn't also charge him with criminal incompetence.

My mum got about ten years older, but she also gained a kind of weary stature through the whole ordeal. She found a strength that hadn't been called on for years. Her and Dad were closer than I've ever seen them. He was forced to come to terms with his own failings, even if he couldn't do too much about them. Maria just grew and grew.

Her and Fred both became real friends of mine for the first time, simply because we spent time together. I can't say I know much about children, but he seems better than most. Well behaved, polite, intelligent, independent and free from the kind of cloying cuteness that most kids seem to have imposed on them by adults. Not only that, but he was good fun.

Maria and I actually sat and talked like we'd never talked before; in fact, we hadn't talked before. I told her about my desires, my friendships and my pleasures, and she made me understand, not without considerable difficulty, that other people could have other desires, other ways. Hers were real and vivid. And when the whole thing was over and my brother was banged up and the glass had come down, Maria announced that she and Fred were going to live in Spain with a man named Xavier who did something in business and loved her dearly.

She told us over Sunday lunch (a ritual I'd only just returned to), and it was all tears and joy in the cranberry jelly. There were real feelings, and I wished her so well. Mum was a bit sad, but showed her strength by recognizing how strong and good Maria was.

'Fred can support Fulham and Barcelona,' Maria said to me, 'and you can come and visit us.'

And I knew I would.

To tell you the third story I must go back a little.

It was in that period when I was still starving for knowledge that Paul and I met. Paul was in his first year at Oxford and hating it. Born and battered in a council estate just behind the Tottenham Court Road, he was the essence of the London boy. As a result, he found all the dreamy spires and dopey squires of Oxford 'as dull as an Arsenal double side, slow as a Spurs centre-half'.

He'd gone to Corpus Christi because he was gifted at history and knew it. But he spent most of his time bunking the train back to Paddington in order to play in the real world. He was a 'capitalist' in that he loved the capital as his own; in fact, when you met him, you knew it was his. On the day we first met he was in a mood that I can only describe as 'considered euphoria'. That was precisely the mood he exuded every day we spent together. He shone.

I don't say that because he was called and known as Diamond, but because he did. He was one of those people who made you feel excited to be with them. It wasn't that you'd call him a genius or treat him with any exaggerated, porcelain respect. He was wildly profane and prone to temper tantrums. He could dance like a dervish (rumour had it he could also fight demons and win, though I never saw him throw a punch), and go for days without sleep of any kind. He was funny and he could control a room. He had heavy traces of misogyny and trouble dealing with the middle classes, whom he hated with every penny of his passion. He had a terrible haircut and he was as tight as a bad mussel. I loved him very quickly and very much and I still do.

And he liked me. Considering his impeccable background, he was strangely lacking in anything approaching taste. At first I think that's what I gave him. He'd tell me all about the People's Rebellion of 1381 and 'why Marxism as an analysis of alienation and labour is now serving to hold the working classes back'. I'd tell him he was a wanker for wearing Fiorucci jeans. Personally, he taught me morality. Most of all, though, what Diamond taught all those who came close to him was that things can be just as right and joyous and perfect as they seem. 'It's up to you, you can do whatever you want' is the thing I remember him saying most.

You might have guessed by now that Paul Diamond is dead. The exact circumstances surrounding how and why Paul Diamond is dead are still something of a mystery. Not just a moral mystery, though if any god is making these decisions, he made a very wrong one. No, what is strange and so difficult to accept is that none of us saw him go. One minute he was Lord Protector of the Pleasure Inc. realm and holding court nightly in the bars of the capital. The next he wasn't.

The actual details are that Paul was in Paris, mixing business with pleasure, as he had done every day of his life, when he had an asthma attack and died. The man was twenty-three years of age, for fuck's sake. Apart from occasionally hearing an inhaler whirr in a bathroom when we shared a hotel, none of us ever knew that he suffered from asthma.

He never discussed it, he never had an attack, and then we hear that he's dead.

Coming from vaguely market-trader stock, he didn't exactly have the physique of an intellectual, nor at times the manner of one. But he had a mind like molten gold. Picture a boy of twenty who could stand on a dancefloor at three in the morning and entertain a crowd of, say, a dozen people with caricatures of eighteenth-century English politicians. I've seen him do it. I've also seen him humble the most gross of music-biz millionaires with a single phrase. I've watched the boy inspire the insolent and fire up the timid. He'd pick you up with just a smile and for five years he was a constant pleasure to be with. He was a man without doubt.

And for all of us he was like an axle round which our friendships revolved. We never revered him. He was a kid called Diamond who liked gold chains and girls with no brains, and he could be wrong just like the rest. But he understood friendship and this world in which we look for the crack better than any man alive. His death hurt me. I hope it hurt us all.

But his parents, or at least what was left of them, didn't seem too bothered. It is a total mystery where Paul got his dignity from; he seems to have been produced by a pair of shadows. Maybe I'm just too bitter about his going, and maybe they were just too tired, too shocked to handle it. But they didn't seem angry or sad, just empty and vaguely pleased, when I took his death away from them. 'We'll celebrate Paul's death our way; his way,' I said. And so we did.

There's no denying the sadness that hung over us all. It was like a mist that obscured all sense of time, that made your face and your mind wet with tears inside and out, tears that never seemed to dry. But there was also a clarity that I will never forget. All of us acted with an efficiency and an economy that was seamless. There was a sense of camaraderie, of unity that Paul himself would have been proud of. My main memory of that time is of hugging people a lot. We were his family and we were going to honour him as well.

The first problem was that Diamond was a devout atheist, who would no more want a foreign god dangled over his death than he'd let one play any part in his life. But how do you go about arranging a secular ceremony? Grandmother Ross's very Catholic funeral was my only experience of organized death, and that didn't help much. He didn't like Scotch eggs any more than he did God. I found out that there were a couple of cemeteries in London where you can be buried on unconsecrated ground, with no deists present: Golders Green and Putney. Or else you can be cremated and have your ashes scattered most anywhere you fancy. But they did say that if you want them poured on water it must be tidal, so the Serpentine was out. Paul hated the suburbs – as far as I know he never ever went to Putney or Golders Green in his entire life. So I didn't think he'd fancy either of those in his death. So we decided (his parents decided to leave it up to us) to have our friend cremated and scatter his ashes in a way that he would enjoy. We were going to have a party too.

We put the word round London that Diamond – not just one of ours, but the best of ours – was going to have a final flourish. Joe and Gabriel came up with a lot of the ideas. Paul would be cremated quietly by people who do that sort of thing. But after we would hold a service of a kind at HQ, carrying his ashes through Soho in a procession down to the Thames, where he would be presented to the winds over Waterloo Bridge. Let the river take him where it will.

That morning our bit of Soho was packed to ripping with people, many of whom hadn't seen a morning in years. All proud and pristine and terribly, terribly sad. In strict Pleasure Inc. tradition we'd informed the police of the precise details of our plans and they were wonderful, cordoning streets and diverting traffic. We never asked for people to wear black or to bring flowers. But by eleven o'clock Meard Street was shoulder to shoulder with pedantically sombre mourners and death lilies lined the kerb.

Standing quietly, hands clasped behind their backs, was every nocturnal face that ever was, each one tight with grief. There were music-biz enemies and old schoolfriends. Mates like Mac and Dave, the Neandersoul Man, and Fran, and Dangerous Jane. There were characters like Albert, the behemoth, and Thin Anthony, dressed in their very finest. Fans of the Sex Bastards came and curtailed their screaming. Club punters who'd paid every time for their pleasures now came to pay their respects. There were pop stars and inebriated writers, the singing girl, photographers, a prince (in disguise, of course), children of the aristocracy, a pair of leading academics, criminals, a group of hardened dope-fiends, who'd taken nothing as a sign of deep respect, top models and topless models, a one-legged man, six make-up artists and girls who carried a torch. For he had laughed with them, even though he had never been able to tell them truly that he loved them. Then there was us, those who loved him most.

His family, both of them, sat inside the Pleasuredome, their car coats done up tight, their knees held tight together, saying nothing. We organized.

Me and Rose, who flowered that day, sharp as a razor and soft as a prayer; Joe, holding it all together, but holding my hand the whole time; Jimmy, who cried like a baby, and kept repeating Paul's name over and over; Gabriel, brooding, quiet. Somehow I suspect he felt a kind of guilt, like he never loved Diamond enough, never got as close. Then there was Little Anthony. His father gone, he stood straight and magnificent in a black three-piece wool-and-cashmere suit with two-inch turnups, which he had made specially for the occasion. And what an occasion.

Inside our velveteen dream of a club, as many as could crowd in and stay noble stood to hear the telegrams, the tributes and the talk, read by our beloved attorney. Diamond, a man of twenty-three years, not even twenty-four, was loved in seven languages and more ways. There was nothing florid or fancy, just bucketloads of respect. And at twelve we moved.

The funeral procession was led by professional mourners – mutes and wailers in full garb – and a pair of ceremonial horses, who knew great repose and looked neither to the left nor the right. In the first hearse were his mother and father, silent, bewildered. The second was for Pleasure Incorporated, the third and fourth for close friends and distant lovers. After that there was a stream of cars stretching the length of Wardour Street.

As we wound our measured, mournful way through the streets, the tenderloin began to say its goodbye. Amusement arcades stopped buzzing, neon blinked and died, whores stopped whoring and pimps stopped hustling. The café owners and the publicans, the tramps, the Chinese and the Maltese stepped out to look and drop their heads. Many of them knew Paul; he loved the place he called 'the neighbourhood' with a proselytizing passion. Many, I guess, didn't, yet still they could not fail to be impressed. Sitting in the back of a big black car, Joe holding my hand and Jimmy weeping uncontrollably on to my shoulder, I looked out and felt glad. Burning, bursting glad that we were doing it well.

Then as we turned the corner into Soho Square, I cried out loud at what I saw. Lined in perfect formation, all the way round the square, were gleaming, glowing bikes, each of them bearing an angel in full regalia, each with a black armband, each bareheaded to the wind. And at their head was one Daniel Marney, old friend. As the hearses reached the exit past CBS Records, the scene of so many of Diamond's greatest battles, Marney was standing to attention on his bike. He saluted our car and beamed a wondrous, contagious smile. We had an escort.

The drive to the river was a blur. A slow-motion, images-melting-together blur, clouded by all the emotions battling to gain control. It felt to me like we were in a film, one of those dream sequences in black and white. It was like we were simultaneously watching and being watched, which, of course, we were. Cameras, the shutters of the curious, the spurious and those who will tell lies, clicked and rolled all the way.

At one point I thought what brilliant publicity this all was for Pleasure Incorporated. But I felt badly guilty for thinking of Paul's sending-off in such mercenary terms. I sank deeper into my suit. Then words punctuated the vast silence of the big black car: 'Don't be sad. Diamond would have loved it. He couldn't have come up with a better media scam himself.'

I hadn't said a word to Kelly, but he knew. We all knew deep down this was the right way. We reached the river.

The sight there, by London's finest bridge, with the city going about its messy, muddled, imperfect business on a Wednesday morning in late May, was the best. Nothing else to say. Organic is not a word that I am wont to use, but as that mad, sad, glamorous carnival stood on the bank of the Thames to say goodbye to a friend, it seemed to me that we had grown from it. And looking round, I guess we had.

Paul's parents stood on the bank, their eyes, and, for all I know, their hearts, still empty, staring nowhere. The leading and very excellent mute lifted the urn from the horse-drawn hearse and handed it to Little Anthony; we walked sombrely to the centre of the bridge, turned to the east and waited. All around us the clockwork flotsam of the town passed by, almost oblivious to the beauty, assuming, I suppose, that we were another video in production.

'Ashes to splashes, Diamond to dust.' Just as we were about to commit Paul to the wind, those words came into my mind, and I was tempted to say them out loud. I didn't. Instead, Anthony held the urn out over the creeping waters of the Thames and spoke the words we'd all agreed upon: 'One Father to Another – Shine on, Diamond.'

We all added a goodbye.

Then Anthony tipped the urn up. And at that moment the breeze seemed to drop and the ashes fell slowly and straight to the river below. A tear from each of us joined them; a part of each of us, I know, went with him. And as I turned to face the crowds, I could see there was a jewel in every eye. Even the angels cried that day.

Later, in the wake that raved and raged and cursed its way deep into the dark night, we drowned our sorrows in drink and drowned our drinks in tears. We all reminisced and pledged undying love, and I took Rose to one side and asked her to help me, for truly I felt so small and lost. I told her how much I loved her, how I believed that she was very great and very good. She asked me to explain to her what I really felt for Paul. This, I believe, is what I said: 'The thing that makes me happiest now is that I loved him while he was here, and he knew that. Me and Diamond, we travelled together, we ran and we fell and we learned to share. He had a generosity the like of which I never expect to see again. The thing he shared was the expectation of greatness, the demand to be special, which he bestowed upon us all. He reached so high, he reached so high. Paul Diamond didn't think he lived a short life, and nor do I. But the world is shorter for his leaving.'

Rose held my hand, wiped my eye, smiled and said, 'Paul is gone. But Pleasure, as ever, remains.'

Trust Me. I'm a Scientist

'Trust me. I'm a scientist.'

The boy in the grease-stained black sixties suit and the goatee beard was known to most as the Ersatz Beatnik. But obviously not to the pair of bridge-and-tunnel boys who were disappearing into the toilet with him. Now the Ersatz Beatnik is no more a scientist than he is an existentialist. He deals bad drugs in bad deals to maintain a bad habit, and he's been hounded out of most every decent nightclub in southern England. Tonight, though, he is in my nightclub, and I can't be bothered. If a couple of suburban groovers want to shove Vim up their noses and pay through the nose for the privilege, who am I to deny them their little thrills? I guess they shouldn't really be in here either.

'*Qué pasa?*'

'*Nada.*'

Gabriel and I had taken to talking mock Spanish with each other, as you do. It was usually in those lulls in a night when you haven't got anything real to say. This was definitely a lull; double *nada*.

The Fun-fair was barely a quarter full; there were few faces, and even fewer heads worth talking to. Ever since we'd opened the second club, life had become a little perfunctory. I won't say that we never still had the crack, but more often than not it was away from work, when we could sit and talk and laugh. More often than not we talked of the Diamond.

I realize now that we'd been groping in the dark a little

since he left us. But I was the last to admit it. He would have wanted strength from us, direction, not doubts. The world was always simple to Paul. You had a world-view, an ideal, if you like, and everything you did was towards that. And everything you did had the maximum fun extracted from it along the way. It all seemed so easy when he was around.

But I, for one, was having trouble finding fun in Pleasure. The empire and I still regularly saw the sun set on us, but it was work. We had two permanent palaces now, one-offs and warehouses and the usual agency facilities, but all the same times were tight. Little Anthony and the Bastards (eleventh-best grossing British band last year) had to be handed over to a team of mobile-phone moguls from America, because we simply couldn't handle it any more. We still got a percentage, but the feared attorney kept talking to me about revenue men and flowing cash problems. I was more concerned with the fact that we didn't see our famous kid brother often enough any more.

'Do you fancy a charge?'

Gabriel had reverted to the Queen's English. I followed suit. 'Mad for it. But not if it's the Beatnik's beak.'

'Don't be silly, Tony. I'm not suicidal. I've got a little left from last night. Let's go to the office.'

Walking across the club, with its fifties Americana carny theme, I still felt vaguely proud of us. But I also felt that I could use this charge.

Gabriel led the way up the back stairs into the dark, private warren of unused space, until we came to an unmarked door that he opened with a large set of keys. Switching on the light with one hand and swinging round into a chair, he was going through a well-practised routine. I sat on the other side of the glass-topped table.

Gabriel moved a few printed handouts, took a Marlboro packet from the inside pocket of his Comme des Garçons suit and pulled out a small pink envelope.

'There's not much left. Is anybody coming down, do you know?'

As he talked, Gab scraped a small pile of powder out of the packet and on to the table with his Access card, then licked the square of paper. He divided the pile neatly into two with one flick of the card and then took an empty biro-case off the desk and swiftly snorted one line through it. I swear he didn't look once.

I didn't look twice. 'Andy said he'd be down later. Do you want to go halves?'

Gabriel held the end of his nose and sniffed hard. 'Why not? Let's go downstairs.'

Walking back past the ferris wheel, I felt better, and so did the club. It had an urgency that had been lacking earlier, and we were in a deep and rapid debate on the morality of an all-pace attack. Gabriel, being of Barbadian descent, was full of fervent favour for what I can only call intimidation. I still think that the grace and guile of a lofted, turning ball in flight is one of life's great beauties. I'm twenty-four years of age and a stickler for tradition.

I was feeling just fine, but also feeling that I could feel just finer if Benign Scotch Andy would turn up for work. There's few sadder sights than the end of an envelope. And they always make you wait for more.

Gabriel and I were standing at the back bar with a young American journalist, here to write a piece on swinging London for some magazine I'd never heard of.

'You haven't heard of it?' said the girl with the bleached blonde hair and the dark glasses, with some surprise. 'It's a lot like the *Face*.'

So we proceeded to tell her that Balkan folk music was definitely the next big thing, and clubs on planes, to avoid national licensing laws; the way of the future. I swear she didn't even grin, just wrote it all down and kept leering at

Gabriel. I couldn't be bothered with the hard sell, I wanted the big buy.

I looked round the club to see if any recognized dealers were in. I saw the Beatnik sliming his way out of the powder-room again, and for a second even considered taxing him for a toot of his poison. You're not that desperate, Tony, I thought. But I very nearly was.

The D J (a girl called Deese, who I'd had a little thing with) was playing a samba track that I didn't recognize, and for a minute I danced a lazy, straight-backed shuffle of a dance and thought of nothing. But after a while my brain and my body started doing the thinking for me. And they thought I definitely wanted some more coke.

I wandered to the front of the house. I told myself I wanted to check how we were doing, but I knew I was really going down to see if anybody had arrived. Andy was just walking up to the doors.

I waved him and his little entourage through the door, and we walked up the crooked stairs together, arm in arm. I really like Andy. He's been chopping my hair for years and occasionally chopping lines as a sideline for almost as long. He also keeps the company of some of the most mucky women in the known world. There were two of them with him tonight.

'Tony, this is Tabitha and Becky.'

I stretched out a hand, and the two girls grinned and giggled at the same time. They said, 'Hello', in the kind of cultivated 'county meets cockney' accent that baby Sloanes all employ. The teenage daughters of smart west London love a walk on the wild side before settling down with a chinless chappie. And most of them seem to walk it with Andy.

I've never felt much affection or attraction for Fulham girls in carefully ripped Levis. So I wasn't too disappointed when they let out a high-pitched 'outrageous' and skipped off to dance the western frug to some interminable hip-hop hit. Besides, it gave me a chance to talk to their escort.

'I need a haircut, Andy. When are you working?'

He ran his fingers through my hair, in the way that hair-dressers always do (I'd been cultivating a kind of fop intellectual fringe, but wasn't entirely convinced), and agreed with me, in the way hairdressers always do.

'Yes, it's looking a mess. Come down to the shop last thing Tuesday and we'll go straight from there to a party. There's a new gallery opening in Battersea – be full of women.'

'Mad for it. Are you working tonight as well?'

'Yes, what do you want?'

'One.'

'No problem. Shall we go upstairs or do you want it here?'

'We'll go up to the office, but I've just got to get Gabriel. Wait for me here.'

My partner in Pleasure was still wedged against the bar by the foreign female, who didn't seem to be dedicated solely to his or her business interests. As I approached, she was being common in a divided language, and Gabriel looked confused. She'd used the word 'ball' and I think he was about to start talking cricket again. I rushed in to save him.

'Gab, you got a second?' I prized his prize-fighter form away.

'I think she wants me to give her more than a PR job. I mean, I'd do it for the company, you understand. But Lucy's coming down later and I'll get well nicked.' He looked genuinely worried, poor boy.

'It's all right, I'll pull her off. By the way, I've organized that beak. Take Benign Scotch Andy upstairs – he's over by the boxing booth. I'll see you in a second.'

I simply told the girl that we had an important strategy

meeting and gave her a couple of free-drink tickets. She just shrugged her shoulders and scanned the bar for some other talent to interview. Unfortunately, there wasn't very much of anything there.

I went straight to the stairs and skipped up two at a time, mildly excited by what waited at the top. Just thinking about it gave me a little rush. As I walked in, Gabriel and Andy were seated round the table and Andy was wiping it clean with a roll of kitchen paper, kept in a filing cabinet for precisely that purpose. An envelope was already on the table.

Gabriel opened it, thanked Andy for his fairness and did the honourable thing, by chopping out three large lines. Andy, his Edinburgh accent occasionally poking through, told us a riotous story about a house party he'd been to in Hampshire, which had gone wild. The story ended with the benign one in the bath, with nothing save a crash helmet on his head and a pair of baby Sloanes on his conscience. Andy, truth be told, doesn't have much of a conscience.

We did the lines and gave the man sixty pounds. He thanked us.

We continued talking for a while, enjoying the rush, while Gabriel folded a square of paper into an envelope and divided the gram into two. I put mine in my shirt pocket. It felt good there. I felt good.

The night got better too. A group of friends arrived from some fashion party and we proceeded to have quite a time. The coke kept me going, and come three o'clock I'd gone through mine (not alone, I hasten to add – we were in a group and you cannot be selfish). So had Gabriel.

'Shall we get some more?'

It's the eternal question when a night has gone horribly right, and I was quite pleased that Gabriel was the one who actually asked it. But if he hadn't, I would have. Instead, I said yes. There were nine or ten of us now, so I decided that we'd turn out all the punters and keep the club open for some private afters.

I did a quick survey to see who wanted to chip for some charge, and all were willing, but most were skint. They were carrying plastic, though, and trooped out like lambs to the autobank, chargecards in hand.

Come five o'clock I thought it was probably time to go home. But when someone said that it was 'too late to stop now', it seemed to make sense. Come six o'clock very little seemed to make sense, but I guess I was having a good time. Come seven o'clock I'd spent one hundred pounds of my money and God knows how much of the club's, but I was having a time. My nose hurt, so did my kidneys, but my conscience only ached a little. I must stop doing this, though, especially when I've got meetings with our lawyer at twelve o'clock.

Joe and I, as the two members of the company who were actually taking care of business, had been summoned to the High (and holy) Holborn offices of Quick, Silver and Quick, Solicitors and Legal Agents, buried deep in the old world of the Inns. I'd always enjoyed going to see the sage, even at one hundred pounds per hour. This was my favourite borough of the city, and Nathaniel Curzon Quick, a man who, I believe, began his career as an advocate for the good preacher Wycliffe, was full of invaluable, enjoyable wisdom. This day, though, I was worried.

Joe was already sitting in the high-backed, stern leather chair in the wooden reception when I arrived. We were both early, which was a sure pointer to the fact that we were both edgy. To try and make myself feel a little better, I nipped into the toilet and snorted what little coke I had left. I'd had little sleep and I figured we needed to be pretty sharp. This might help.

Mr Nathaniel Quick has always insisted that we call him Nathan, but first-name terms don't come too easily when a man looks more than a little like the Holy Father. This time, as I shook his hand and gave him a rather nervous 'Good day, Mr Quick', he didn't say a word in protest. Instead he sat straight down behind the massive leather-topped desk and looked his severest look. I just hoped he couldn't see that my hands were sweating.

'Tony, Joe, I'm afraid I must inform you that things are very bad indeed. In the year since Paul's tragic death your expenditure has far outweighed your income. The new enterprises, such as the Fun-fair and that ill-considered Warehouses of the World project, have simply not worked. And you two, along with Gabriel and James, have, as individuals, been paying yourselves more and more. I hope you do not mind me asking, but what in Heaven's name have you been doing with it?'

He didn't wait for an answer, and I prayed he didn't already know.

'Basically, gentlemen, something drastic is going to have to be done. You are wildly overstretched, your creditors are not in a generous mood and you need to raise some money quickly, or else trim the operations drastically. These, I am afraid, are dark days for Pleasure.'

Joe and I looked at each other, looked at Nathaniel Quick, and I looked behind the feared attorney at the portrait of Nathaniel Quick, Senior, who had founded the firm the day after the dawn of time. I think, from the look of his all-seeing eyes, that he knew exactly how I felt and why. There were a million things I wanted to say, and none of them were right, so I just ground my teeth instead.

Joe spoke. 'Mr Quick. I realize that we have made some major mistakes, so tell us exactly what we have got to do to rectify them.'

He nodded slightly and began: 'In the first instance, you must raise some ready capital. A sum of approximately twenty-five thousand pounds is needed straight away to keep the most avaricious wolves from the door. Mind you, that is only a beginning. After that it is about reorganizing, redefining and rediscovering the initial drive and originality which made Pleasure Incorporated such a success and, may I add, such a pleasure to be associated with.'

'How much have we actually got?' Again Joe beat me to a coherent question.

'Well, obviously there is the property, two nightclub complexes. But in terms of liquid assets, including the latest takings, you may have perhaps eight thousand pounds. But wages have to be paid out of that.'

'How long have we got?' I finally stammered something out.

'No more than a week. I have been warning you of this situation for some time, yet my advice seems sadly to have fallen on deaf ears.'

Joe and I just sat silently until the holy man spoke again.

'Look, there is nothing for you to do now, except to go from here and talk it through. My only advice is that you must act decisively or it will all crumble.' With that he rose, shook our hands and ushered us out of our immediate misery.

Leaving the offices, we decided to go round the corner for a drink. My mouth felt like Arizona, and my mind as empty as Montana. We settled on a pub where Joe's father used to drink when he was still on the print, when there were still printers in Fleet Street. Somehow it seemed right to celebrate the end of an era in a ghost town.

In the days of the goldrush there had been big men draped with gold and laden with fat wedges of tens and twenties, taking their place at the bar every morning. The Apprentice used to roar. Now it was empty, save for a couple of Americans who couldn't locate the Cheshire Cheese and a group of old compositors whose drinking habits die hard. My guts felt like they were going to drop at any moment. Joe ordered a couple of drinks.

Apart from my partner saying, 'What are we going to do?' and me replying, 'I don't know', we sat in silence. In order to turn the screw a little and make myself feel even worse, I kept going over the events of the night before. I felt like Nero with a hangover.

Then I suddenly remembered something Benign Scotch Andy had said. He was telling me that there was a shipment coming in from the Continent, and if he could get ten grand, he could more than double it in a few days. It was simply a matter of putting the money up, bank-rolling a shipment, that's all. Eight grand is nearly ten grand.

'Joe, tell me what you think.'

Basically Joe hated the idea. I could see him wince as I said it. But he couldn't think of anything else. He had lots of reservations, but no alternatives. Most of his doubts were about the kind of company we'd have to keep and the precedent that we'd be setting. But I persuaded him that we should put it to the others in a meeting that very evening. Seven o'clock at the Pleasuredome.

I jumped out of the cab at the corner of Oxford Street and Tottenham Court Road. The traffic was terrible round the one-way system, and I decided to walk into Soho. Crossing over into Charing Cross Road, I spotted that they were all there again. Junkies move even more slowly than tortoises and council workers. I know in the sixties they used to crowd round the toilets at Piccadilly Circus. Well, in twenty years, they've gone about 800 yards north to their latest cosy little home, opposite Centre Point by the alley into Soho Square.

Almost every day I see them. Vacant lots, the south Bronx of humanity, just standing and waiting. You can tell when they started doing smack, because that's the last time they bought any clothes. Most of this lot dated to about 1974–6 and looked like they'd been standing out in the cold ever since. As I walked past and caught a couple of unseeing, empty eyes, I had little sympathy. But it's when you see them with their kids, hanging on to their decaying bodies, that it really hits home. They should have the dignity to go and die, but dignity is exactly what they haven't got left.

After turning round into Old Compton Street, I bought a paper off the stand. I buy a paper off that stand every day, and the man has never recognized me once. I glanced at the headlines about some multi-million-pound scandal in the City, and then turned to the back to see if Fulham had bought that goalkeeper from Swindon yet. They hadn't.

I was the first in, but the others soon arrived. Joe and I outlined what Quick had said to us and asked the others if they had any suggestions. Jimmy is a very practical man and he handles all the logistics of our operation, but you don't really expect him to come up with suggestions. He didn't. And Gabriel, well, Gabriel is charming, and that is a talent which has stood us in enormous stead. But we needed more than charm right now. I told them my idea.

Gabriel surprised me by throwing up most doubts. He was very sceptical indeed and seemed almost morally disturbed, which seemed to me to be a little hypocritical, to say the least. Jimmy wanted to make sure that it was all very tightly done and that we weren't going to get ripped off, but basically he was happy. Joe had little to add from the morning, save to say that this could only be a temporary solution, which I thought was pretty bloody obvious. In the end I phoned Andy and asked him to come and meet us.

He was late, of course. It was nearly ten o'clock before he arrived, and the club was getting ready for the night. As soon as he got there, we took him to the office. It wasn't exactly the first time he'd been there, but I'm sure it was the first time we hadn't taken any drugs. We just talked about them.

I told him that we might be interested in investing ten grand in a shipment, provided that it could all be completed quickly and with anonymity guaranteed. Andy would act as our agent and get a percentage. He picked up the phone and dialled a number that I noticed began with a nine.

'Can I speak to Mr Knight? Tell him it's his hairdresser ... Yes ... I think I might be able to take up your latest proposition ... Yes, ten ... As soon as possible ... No.'

He turned and looked at me. 'Can you make eleven o'clock tomorrow morning?'

'Can you?' I said, with some incredulity. I didn't think Andy believed in life before lunch.

He didn't answer me but turned to the phone. 'Yes, we'll be there, two of us at twelve o'clock.'

'All right, Tony, you are going to have to get the cash together first thing tomorrow morning, and I will meet you here at 10.45. I warn you, I will be on time. You don't mess these people about.'

I just nodded.

He smiled. 'Fancy a line to celebrate?'

I just nodded.

I didn't feel nervous that night, simply pleased to have found a lifeline. I must admit, I was also looking foward to finding out what the people were like further up the supply line, to seeing if they really had tails. Rounding up the money meant going to both clubs at the end of the night and physically taking the takings. Joe and Jimmy went to the Fun-fair, and Gabriel and I stayed at the Pleasuredome. I'd had little sleep the night before and wasn't going to get much tonight, so I bought another half, but did it sparingly so as not to get wired. I told myself it was strictly for business.

We had to pay bouncers (you have to pay bouncers), but we knocked everybody else, including the band which had played at the Fun-fair. It could wait. We were still left with nearly two grand, which isn't bad at all for a Thursday night. I put the money in a carrier-bag and called a cab on account to take me home. It was nearly five o'clock, so I would get a few hours' sleep, which isn't bad for a boy of my age. Besides, I still had some coke left to push me up in the morning. I felt quite excited really.

I'd told Rose all about the troubles we were in and about the idea I had for solving them. She wasn't shocked and I wouldn't say she was worried. But she kept saying that money could only buy time, that we had to look deeper. I'd told her that time was exactly what we needed right now, as we were already in so deep that we were close to drowning. She was, understandably, asleep when I got home and still would be when I left, so I slept in the spare bed. It wasn't exactly the first time.

She was still asleep when I left.

The visit to our bank in Holborn went off with far less pain than I feared. Somehow you kind of think that they might know what you're going to do with it. But they just gave me the seven thousand eight hundred and wished me a good day.

I arrived at the club just after 10.30, bought a coffee in a polystyrene cup with a plastic lid from a café over the road and waited. Andy had insisted that he wouldn't be late, and for once I believed him.

He was late.

I chopped a line out for myself, but felt a bit self-conscious doing it. Somehow the night makes things feel right, but now I felt dirty, like I hadn't washed from the night before. Truth be told, I hadn't.

At two minutes past eleven the buzzer rang and the voice of my hairdresser was calling me down. I went straight downstairs, opened the door. Andy was standing there, and a white Escort XR3 was standing behind him with the door open. The Scotsman indicated that I should get in the back.

'Tony, this is Gary.'

I nodded to the boy sitting in the driver's seat. It is not in my nature to trust people who drive cars with white wheels, especially people with south London accents and Gucci shoes. I didn't speak much, despite the coke running around my system. Andy had obviously been imbibing too, because he was wired to hell and rattling on.

As we drove south through the drizzle of a working day, I didn't ask where we were going. I didn't want to appear naïve and somehow it seemed as if I should know. The boy in the front used the Guccis to push the white Escort faster than it should go, and I just prayed that we weren't carrying. I was carrying ten thousand pounds in a Gladstone bag and beginning to feel a little uneasy. Don't get me wrong – it wasn't a question of morality, just taste.

For a while we talked football, and for the first time in my life I was consciously in the company of a Crystal Palace supporter. He wasn't happy when I told him that. He cheered up, though, in Putney and Wandsworth when we got on to the topic of wine bars, which he was something of a connoisseur of. He slowed down in Wimbledon, because we sat behind a panda car. He actually laughed in Surbiton when Andy cracked a hateful joke about Pakis.

I didn't feel like laughing, I felt like going home. I didn't know where we were and didn't know where we were going. By now I was beginning to wonder if we were driving to the Continent to get the stuff ourselves. I was coming down sitting in the back of a white car, feeling at the same time much older than I am and far younger than I'll ever be again.

'We're here.'

It was just another of those streets, between the ghetto and the sea, that you get if you keep going south. Tree lined and totally detached, it was where the home counties call home, what they call the affluent south-east. I'd never really been to the affluent south-east before and I wasn't impressed.

Somehow it just wasn't what I expected, it wasn't like the movies – a lock-up in Docklands or a penthouse in Mayfair, perhaps – but a glorified Barratt's home in what I assumed was Surrey. That's the worst kind of sleazy, the kind people don't sing about. Still, I kept on telling myself, we need the money. It was, I'll admit, a consoling thought.

As we got out of the car, I realized that our chauffeur was no older than me, probably a little younger. He was short, built like a terrier and ugly, very ugly. I'm sorry, but I don't like ugly people, people who are ugly on the inside.

'Andy, what the fuck are we doing?'

The Crystal Palace fan had knocked on the door, with its carriage lamps, and was entering just ahead of us, so I had to whisper.

'Chill out. Gary is the man I usually deal with, but we've got to go one higher. I've never been here before, but it'll be fine.'

It was the kind of house that I've always assumed personnel managers live in. All thick carpets and nearly real knick-knacks that cost a lot of money but aren't worth any. It was a house with too many things in it and none of them were even slightly broken. I felt even less at ease than I had in the white car.

I was clutching the bag tight as we were led into the big beige sitting-room and asked by the balding, late-thirties man who'd opened the door if we'd like coffee. There were two other young entrepreneurs sitting in the room; and it felt tense, or at least I felt tense. I would have much preferred it if we could have simply got the business over and done with. But then, you always have to wait.

It was filter coffee, and one of the most disturbingly surreal scenes I've ever been involved in: sitting in this over-made-up suburban living-room, making polite conversation and waiting for nobody seemed to know what, with ten grand wedged between my knees and a bone-china cup on top of them. The balding man was called Robert and he didn't have an accent. I assumed we were waiting for the man.

After about fifteen minutes of this tea-with-vicar tension, there was a ring from the front door and Robert got up to answer it. A moment later he returned with a boy in a grease-stained black sixties suit and a goatee beard. My soul sank.

I felt as grubby as the suit that weasel always wears, just by being in the room with him. He grinned his meaningless junkie grin at me and let out a little 'welcome to the leper colony' laugh. Robert introduced him as Julian. I always thought his mother had christened him Ersatz.

Robert spoke and I was amazed. He was the man.

'OK, then, gentlemen. I understand that you are all desirous of investing in my merchandise.' He smiled like an accountant. 'The procedure is this. I will show you a sample of the goods on offer, and, believe me, it is the finest available.' Another smile. 'If you are satisfied as to its quality, you will then give me the money, and the consignment, including your percentage, will arrive tomorrow and be distributed by Monday, when you can collect your return, minus my handling charge, of course.'

'How do we know that we will ever see the money again?' It seemed such an obvious question, yet somehow I felt almost guilty for asking it. Robert, who I suddenly realized looked a little like a younger Paul Eddington, looked right at me and looked hurt.

'Trust me. I'm a businessman. These other gentlemen, who are regular customers, will, I'm sure, vouch for me. But to allay any doubts I will make out a cheque for the precise amount you invest from my company account. This is an entirely legitimate business, which you can check at Companies House. But the fact that they are Coutts cheques should be guarantee enough. Now, if you will wait one second.'

He left the room and returned almost immediately, carrying a small silver snuff-box. I felt horrible in every sense; I didn't particularly want to be part of this. But the thought of a test toot had its appeal, and in the end there was only one pertinent fact. We needed the money.

First in the line was the fake Beatnik. He looked in the box, then dipped his finger in, smiled and tasted a tiny sample. Then he took a small coke-spoon out of his pocket and expertly sniffed a sample up each nostril. The smile grew and he congratulated our host on the quality of his 'gear'.

I was next, and the box was proffered with an almost dainty politeness. As soon as I opened it, I saw there was something wrong. Instead of gleaming, white crystals this was a golden, brown powder. It couldn't be cocaine, but still I tasted it, thinking that maybe I was seeing wrong. Instead of a clean, numbing taste there was a sweet, slightly burnt flavour.

'What's that?' I turned my head from our host to Andy and back.

'That, my dear boy, is the finest uncut Indian heroin. What did you expect – sherbet?'

'I expected cocaine,' I said, looking at Scotch Andy, who just shrugged. Then I turned to the balding one. I hated that man, oh, how I hated that man.

'Then I am afraid you were ill-informed. Still, it makes no difference to you. If you are not qualified to judge this batch, then I am sure Julian will testify as to its quality. And besides, you will not even see it, so it makes no odds.'

He was right, of course. What difference does it make to me if it's smack, crack or pot? It isn't my breakfast. The money is all that matters.

'We will sell anything except our souls.' It wasn't a voice from beyond or anything like that, it was just a memory. It was a memory of a boy I loved, who loved morality. He said that to me once, and I suddenly knew that I couldn't sell his soul to save our Pleasure.

'I'm sorry, but I am afraid that I am going to have to withdraw from the transaction. No offence intended and no aspersions cast. But I do not want to be involved.' I grasped the bag even tighter, fearing the worst. And indeed Crystal Palace, who'd been sitting on the other side of the room, stood up and squared up. He looked at Robert, as if to take orders, but Mr Robert just shook his head.

'That, of course, is your prerogative. As I said before, I am a businessman, and if you do not wish to do business, so be it. I hope, though, that I can trust you to respect the confidentiality of this occasion. I don't have to tell you that it would not be wise to do otherwise.'

I felt a wonderful elation standing in the middle of that fussy, fetid room, felt tall for the first time in a long time. I offered my hand to Mr Robert. 'Trust me. I'm a friend of Paul Diamond's.'

There weren't any other magic solutions. The contents of the Gladstone bag were given straight back to the bank, who then gave it straight to the multitudes that we owed money to. We had to sell the Fun-fair (I never liked it anyway), close the agency and severely curtail our lifestyles. It was a hard winter when I was twenty-four, but Fulham avoided relegation, and so, I guess, did we.

There was a time when it was close, though, when the Pleasuredome and the Pleasure dream itself were under siege. But a Sex Bastards' royalty cheque arrived on a white charger and just about saved the day. Things were hard for Rose and me too. She thought I was taking too many drugs, I thought she was taking too little interest, but we've come through it now. I think things could be better than ever.

And things were much better between us boys. It fits all the clichés, but we felt like a family again. We were in the bunker, backs to the wall and all that, and it worked. It was a battle to keep going, but we gained energy from every encounter. What is the opposite of battle-weary? Well, whatever it is, we had it, and it was good to feel. My brother, who I went to see every now and then, was doing just fine, dealing dope on his wing. He was sending home twenty-five quid a week to my mum, which made me chuckle. He'd finally found the thing in life he could do better than me.

I will also admit I laughed just a little when the feared attorney with the religious gait announced that he was leaving his wife and setting up home in Docklands, with a 24-year-old girl he met in the Pleasuredome. We all laughed actually, but wished them both well and meant it.

And when the dirt had cleared and we were still standing, Joe and I decided to go on a trip for fun and profit, which I guess is the only kind. So we phoned Mr Costa and went to Gatwick. Bound for the cubic city.

Part Two

To the Cubic City

Part two of this book begins on an aeroplane, where our bruised but unbroken boy, now twenty-four years of this world, sits. He has managed, by the sheer power of will, to secure two first-class seats on the Virgin Gatwick to Newark, upgraded, by the favours of a friend, from the Apex fares actually paid for. He is accompanied by his ginger *compañero* of some eight summers' standing, and the two are lounging in the stolen luxury of their accommodation and drowning in the freeness of the champagne, a drink which they both agree always tastes better when you do not have to pay for it. Taken by the joy of the situation, our boy breaks into a lengthy monologue about the city that awaits them at the end of their flight, a city that has been filmed and photographed, spoken and sung about so often that its reputation stands higher and more daunting than any of its skyscrapers. When he gets to the part where they name it twice, his mate, who'd actually been there, feels honour bound to interject, 'Bollocks.'

'What?'

'That's absolute bollocks.'

'What is?'

'The idea that New York is some kind of rock-hard training school that can't be beaten. Don't get me wrong, I love the place, but it's piss-easy compared to London, it's just had better PR, that's all. Remember, Tony, all towns are small towns − don't allow yourself to be daunted by it. We'll walk it over there. We're grown-ups, Tony, we've got traditions and we've got taste, which is something they can never, for all their bluster, argue with. Enjoy it, but don't get taken in, mate. Remember when you're walking down one of those avenues, and it feels like a canyon in the centre of the universe, that you are just off the coast of the moral majority, so hold your head high; we're selling England.'

I looked at Kelly and I could tell from his eyes that he really meant it, bless him. So I just nodded. 'All right, Joe,' I said.

The remainder of the flight was taken up with musing on the Manhattan that awaited and with an Agatha Christie I'd bought at the airport. I've always preferred Miss Marple, but I'd picked up a Poirot and stuck with it. By the time the 'Fasten Seat-belts' signs were on, I'd figured out that it was Inspector Crome who was committing the horrible ABC murders and leading poor Poirot such a merry dance. But then, the champagne was very free.

And then suddenly I wished it hadn't been. My stomach started to my throat as our aeroplane began to dive towards the ground. For a few seconds I experienced that awful, swollen, expectant feeling of real fear. Then we hit the tarmac with a double bump and a burst of applause from the economies below. I breathed out a burst of the by now pretty stale air and tried to cram my bloated feet back into a pair of brogues as we taxied to a halt.

As I walked groggily down the steps and out past the inanely grinning hostesses, the relief and fatigue were mixed with a powerful, imposing sense of anticipation. New York to me is the great metropolitan myth, the vicarious vision I've had a host of times. Joe can be blasé because he's been there before, but I wanted to feel excited. This was Gotham City, for fuck's sake, just a baggage reclaim away.

Airports all sound the same. It's that busy, sonorous, echoing sound of overworked machines and tempers, both on the edge of breaking point from too many languages and not enough time. But somehow as we shuffled through the mêlée, towards the passport control, it all seemed at one remove; as if we were in a bubble coasting above it to some kind of easy confrontation with a destiny that was now decided. Or at least that's how it seemed to me.

After all the horror stories I'd heard about American immigration, I expected a grilling. But a stern black lady in a sweat-stained blue shirt, who seemed loaded with grief, looked at my visa (unlimited) and my photograph (unrecognizable), stamped her stamp and said in a voice I'd heard on the TV, 'Have a nice stay.' Kelly was already through and he beamed at me with all the excitement he'd been holding back throughout the flight.

'Somebody call me a checker,' he drawled in a plastic accent.

'You're a fucking checker, Kelly,' said I.

'That's as may be,' said he. 'But remember what I said.'

'You said, let's get a cab. So let's get one.'

He put his arm round my shoulder and gave it a squeeze. It's not easy to walk arm in arm holding suitcases in a new country. But we gave it a go.

As we strolled out of the artificial atmosphere of the airport and into the air of America, the heat hit home, knocking me out of my bubble for a second. Now we were part of the mayhem and the muddle of businessmen and tourists and travellers and people returning from conventions in Hawaii, all scrambling about with bags and trolleys, hustling for buses and cabs, asking questions and receiving no replies. For a moment I wished for all my worth that we could get a whisk, get some kind of VIP treatment to cut through this mess and carry us straight to the clarity of the city. I wanted neon shining bright.

'Mr Kelly and Mr Ross?'

We both spun round to face the voice and saw a tall, officious-looking man in a grey suit a size too small for him, who stood as if he knew about the world. My first response was to go straight into auto-lie and deny it. But he obviously knew exactly who we were.

'Yes, that's us,' said Joe.

'What is it?' said I.

My mind was racing like a computer on crack, through a series of options. I'm not paranoid, but it went: Customs, drugs, Communism (Joe had once been a member and I had an East German stamp), visas, money, some kind of stitch-up. I even considered the possibility that Mr Robert had decided to take umbrage after all and had had a word with some Mafia mates. All these thoughts went through my head in the time it took Clint Eastwood in front of us to answer.

'Will you please accompany me, sirs?' said he.

'Why?'

'Because I have asked you to.'

My head was spinning. First landing, now this. I could see that Joe was contemplating swinging or running, and it didn't look wise. So I grabbed his arm and tried to keep him calm by sounding it myself. 'Could you please tell us what all this is about?'

'If you will just follow me a few yards, sir, you will soon find out.'

I picked up my case and nodded at Joe to do the same. This gorilla was not going to let us ignore him, and he obviously wasn't programmed to respond to reason. As we picked up the bags, he began to take terrifying John Wayne steps that we almost had to run to keep up with. Neither of us said a word as we walked, mute through fear. But our guide and captor led us past a row of limos waiting for the stars to come out, to the biggest, blackest, darkest-windowed car I've ever seen. Suddenly he stopped, opened one of the doors and beckoned horribly for us to enter.

What do you do? I figured it had to be the Mafia. It was just like the movies, only I'm not in the movies, I'm in real life. It was so unreal that I started to laugh. I think the next stage of the fear would have been shit running down my legs. I could already feel the muscles of my stomach let go, when suddenly out of the blind darkness of the car something leapt at us, screaming. I dropped the bag and tried to react, but it was on top of me. And just as the arms went round my neck, I realized that I was being attacked by a bubble. It was fucking Little Anthony, the Barbarian Sex Bastard himself. And what a bastard indeed.

'Tony, Joe, you wankers.'

The mix of relief, annoyance and sheer pleasure made for the most intoxicating cocktail of surprises, and I didn't really know whether to shout at him, kiss him or kick him; so I think I did all three. Joe did the same and we all ended up rolling round on the floor in an incoherent ruck.

'What the fuck are you doing here, and what the fuck was that all about?' I asked as we finally struggled to our feet.

Joe hugged him and said, 'You're meant to be in the Bahamas, recording at Compass Point, aren't you?'

'That there was just my little joke, and I can see it worked. Nassau I blew out for a few weeks. My big brothers' coming to town takes priority over making a pop record that the world can well wait for. Oh, and by the way, this is Lou, my minder and driver.'

Anthony, with his broadest smile, introduced the broadest man. Our man in a suit smiled and proffered a massive hand. We both shook it. I was still shaking inside.

'That was a fucking stupid stunt, Anthony. I nearly shit myself,' I said, trying to look stern.

'Shut up, dad, and get in the car. You two have got a city to see. The next two weeks will probably kill you anyway.'

Uncurling into the massive car, I remembered that the last time we'd all sat in a limo together was at Paul's funeral. But I decided that it was best to keep my sadness to myself rather than tear the happiness that had wrapped itself around us all again. I chose instead to look at my young friend, dressed in a chocolate-brown matador-style suit that I would guess he'd had made specially for the occasion. I had a suspicion Joe was thinking the same thoughts, because he too was silent and staring.

Mr Costa wanted to talk. He sounded grown-up; I guess he *had* grown up. Funny that.

'How in the world have you been? I've missed you both with all my love. Tell me everything. All this living-in-exile lark makes you distant. How's Jimmy and Gabriel? How's Pleasure Inc.? Why didn't you tell me you were getting grief about money? I might be away, but I hear things, you know. How's the crack in London?'

All these questions were thrown out as we rolled un-noticeably in our tank away from the airport and towards New York. It felt warm and safe and sure to be with our kid again. I didn't really feel like answering questions, so Joe did most of the answering. I wanted to be overwhelmed by Manhattan. I wanted to see the hanging Gardens of Babylon. Then suddenly there it was.

The first impression is, I've seen it before. Because, of course, you have, we all have a thousand times. And then you look again and you know you've never seen anything like it before. It's so big, so unreal, unthinkably big, and so fine. From a distance, in a big car, it looks like a canvas painted with metallic, flowing lines by an imagination so vast and desperate and foolhardy that it set out to deny and defy all the forces that nature can throw. And then as you come closer and you begin to sense its anger and its pride at being made such a monster, it stops being a skyline and it becomes, most unbelievably, a city. Which makes it even more a thing of wonder and awe. So that you want it to swallow you whole. You want to explore its insides like some Jonah who thinks himself lucky to be in the belly of this creation of man; this cubic city.

All of this they let me think in silence, these friends of mine, until we had entered the city walls and could no longer see how imposing its towers are. Then Anthony spoke to me in all my wonderment. And this is what he said: 'That will happen every single time you see that sight. The strangest, strongest thing about the power of that vision is that it never fades. With that scene, my brother, familiarity breeds only addiction. But be warned. This island is a miasma of narcotic gases in which you can dream and float to your heart's easy content. You can just let New York happen to you, you can dream here for ever. But you must not if you wish to tame her.'

At least, that is what I heard and understood of what he said. We were also told that, instead of at the Gramercy Park Hotel as we had planned, we would be staying in the vacant home of one Mr Bernie Weinstock. He is a nightclub entrepreneur friend of the Sex Bastards and was only too pleased to leave us the keys to his loft on 14th and 2nd. Little Anthony was renting an apartment about ten blocks north for exorbitant amounts, so we would be close.

As the car weaved through the claustrophobic crosstown traffic of a muggy Monday, I listened to this, trying to soak up all the talk of ups and downs and 33rds and 3rds, along with the vivid television programme passing in front of my eyes outside the car.

We stopped.

It was mid-afternoon in Manhattan in July, and there was a pervading air of what I can only describe as empty expectancy as we tumbled out of the limousine and on to the street. A huddle of black and hispanic guys of indeterminate age were just hanging over the block, and they gave us a few whistles as we unloaded. From some of the stares, I felt glad that we had Lou with us. But somehow it didn't seem that heavy, just kind of dull and edgy, as if everyone was waiting for something to happen, but was too lazy to do anything about it.

Anthony had the keys, and with some trouble he opened a nondescript-looking door next to a grocer's shop that was spilling on to the street. Once inside he called a metal lift that was right inside the door, telling us all the time about this neighbourhood: how it was funky but fine, but how it was best not to buy drugs off the street or we'd get hustled for business. He's been living in the city on and off for the best part of a year now, because the Bastards are big here, and he seemed to know it pretty well. His considered opinion was: 'The place is hard, but the people are pretty soft, and there's certainly times and money to be had.' That sounded just dandy.

The apartment was – well, wonderful. A massive open space, about half the size of a football pitch, with nothing in it save everything you've ever wanted, but still with room to wander lonely. All it needed was a resident Chinese girl on roller-skates, and I would gladly have signed to stay inside her walls for ever. But instead I decided to go straight out. Anthony had some work to do and arranged to meet us later for dinner. Joe wanted to phone some old friends and get some rest. I wanted to look and learn.

Like most reputations, I was sure that New York's was based on fact but exaggerated beyond sense. I can't say I was scared. I'd been given enough briefings on where not and who not and how not. But then, back home I've been to football matches where you could be murdered because of the colour of your hat and discos where you daren't look at a girl for fear of a glass in your eye. We're incredibly hypocritical about violence. There is probably more irrational violence in nice, cosy, working-class Britain than there is anywhere in the world. That's what I told myself as I pulled my boots on and prepared to dive in.

I began to walk. Just wandered. Past the Disco Donut where twenty-four hours a day you could buy the best burgers in all New York, or so the neon said. Past the sex cinema that looked like it had body-positive walls. Past town criers with their bored mantras: 'reefer, coke, crack'. Past the Korean delis with their multi-coloured fountains of fruit and vegetables. Past dry-cleaners' warehouses and men in neat short-sleeved shirts. Past drunks and probably corpses, past policemen swinging batons and wiping brows, past the holes in the ground that seemed to lead to hell or the subway or both.

I was really going now, strutting past bars that boasted the shamrock and boys that just boasted. Past madness and ordinary life, and I could feel what the fuss was all about, feel the energy of the city, which was so strong that it sapped the strength of its people the moment they weakened, but which right now was giving me a massive charge. I looked up and saw the Empire State, and it took my breath away in a gently old-fashioned sort of way. And then there was the Chrysler Building and the cabs and the steam that rose so prettily from Hades below. And all the while I walked and watched and felt not at home but certainly at ease. And then I decided on a drink.

In a dark bar with maybe five other fellows, I drank a beer and watched advertisements and the news on the television and got asked where I was from three times. I also got told that the Mets were heading for a pennant this year, that the mayor was a crook and that I should be careful because it is a hungry world out there. And all in all I encountered such manners as I found truly pleasing. And when I decided to stroll back to 14th and 2nd, I was wished a very fond farewell. A spell was being woven no doubt, but I was sure that I could catch it and use it as a charm. It felt like one of those days when I was young.

That night we met in a restaurant called the Cat House, which was styled like a New Orleans brothel and served Creole Cumbos in wooden booths to those who wished to be conspiratorial and chic. Fronted by the fat lady, it was buried deep in the Alphabet, which, I was told, had once been the worst war zone in all the city and which still bore the human scars of its recent history. The shells of people littered the streets like so many burnt-out tanks on a battlefield, such was the volume of victims. It seemed to me a very sad *barrio*. But that, I soon learned, was the way of their world.

At first the three of us just sat and stretched out memories and gossiped awhile. But it wasn't like old friends. It was like now friends, like it should be. Little Anthony told us how Paul's death had made him want to hide for a time in the anonymity of pop-stardom, but how he now felt alive again. I told him about the escapade of the chameleon cocaine that never was, and he laughed out loud and told me I was stupid for pulling out. But I don't believe he meant it.

Joe told him the details of the Pleasure problems, but also about how we had saved it and still had Meard Street and a reputation that was rising again, especially after London fashion week, which we handled well and, indeed, made money from. He also told him the tale of the religious attorney and the riverside love-nest, which forced our friend to giggle into his grits. Then he asked us what our plans were, and we said we planned England.

The idea was simple. Pleasure Incorporated, the world-famous, London-based purveyor of sweet delight, would sell the streets of England to the sidewalks of America. Given the current interest in all things swinging London and the widespread ignorance about what is really going on in the land of hype and glory, we will help. You want an English video director or D J? Producer or designer? Stylist or star? Call us. You want that suit you saw in the *Face* but don't know where to get it? Call us. You want to know tomorrow's trend today? You want to stay in London but don't know where to go? You want that invitation? That phone number? That address? You just must have that male model with the mohican at your party. Phone us: phone England.

We will be the beefeaters of the towers of trendy London, the fixits of fabdom, who can sell you the right stuff, because, of course, we are the right stuff. The plan is to set up an agency in New York, and then a shop selling all things intrinsically of our England. With luck they will be the first of a few, trading, as we say, in all aspects of the new England. And the name will be England.

'Anthony, where do we begin?'

He looked pretend pensive for a second and then grinned. 'Where do all things begin? With a party, of course.'

To celebrate we ordered the house speciality, a Zydeco Delight. This was a sumptuous confection that consisted of various sorbets and meringues with pistachios and plantains, syrups, syllabubs and salt, topped with cherry cream, always served by the fat lady herself as a sign of respect.

After that we drank four Tequila Slammers. This is a drink executed by filling a shot glass with equal measures of gold-label tequila from down Mexico way and dry champagne from the fields of old France and then slamming the glass three times on a suitable counter, thereby exciting the bubbles and all present. You then drain the glass in one and get very drunk and have much fun.

And all the while we did this we discussed the details of our hoe-down. It would be an English party, staged and staffed and stuffed with all the useful English expats and experts on the island. It would be designed to wind up the locals by making it exceedingly difficult for them to secure entry, unless, of course they were nice to us, and even then probably not. If a success, it would show that we had the know-how and that we knew who. 'Besides,' Joe said, between the third and fourth of the slammers, 'we'll have a laugh.'

But to begin even the beginning, we had first to go out.

Now clubs are clubs. Of course, I was excited about my first foray into the city that never lets you sleep. But night-club culture is a cosmopolitan culture, and I didn't expect too many surprises. Within five minutes of pulling 'can pay, won't pay' at a downtown boy-bar called Darkness, I felt completely in command. Apart from the fact that more money had obviously been spent on the décor, it felt like home, only less so. I'm used to élitism, and it soon became obvious that everybody from hippies to Yuppies is allowed to play, as long as they can pay their way. They even let in decent respectable people. That came as a sad surprise.

After Darkness we went to Moll Flanders, a swish, swing-ing, singing bar fronted by Edie, a svelte French chanteuse. Then to the Cockpit, a lowly dive-bar of high repute, where the night did, I must admit, kick up a gear. Then forward to a disco called Swans, where all three of us danced a mean mashed potato to old J B and caused a storm by so doing. Then to Tango to tango and finally to the Abattoir, the latest and rarest and, so they said, most exclusive of them all. And, of course, we waltzed it. Here I was impressed by the sheer effort involved in creating a disco that looked like 'The Fall of the Roman Empire Meets *Metropolis* in Dis-neyland'. But still the crowd didn't really cut it.

But all along we met people. Some of them were old faces from London town, whom I knew vaguely or well. But best of all we met Fran from the old Boomtime days. She was delirious to see us (she was also plain delirious because she had taken an entire collection of designer drugs). There were too some local friends of Anthony's and Joe's, and faces from Paris and Berlin. All of them seemed pleased that we were here. And all in all and all along I was impressed. But not very.

Then we wound down in Save the Robots, an illegal 'after hours' much frequented by narcotics dealers and pimps and such gentlefolk of the night as we were used to meeting in the mornings. And come sufficient time, we decided we had done a good day's work. So we celebrated with home fries and waffles and Canadian bacon, orange juice, coffee and soda (alternatively known as Number Five Combo) in Dave's Diner, where Mr Sinatra himself, we were assured, had eaten the self-same breakfast.

And then to bed.

The next couple of days were spent familiarizing ourselves with the town, and it with us, paying special attention, of course, to the English, of whom there were many. We even took a carefully selected few into our confidence, knowing naturally that they would tell no one, and everyone, of our plans. Then, when we had visited all the choicest cuts, all the clubs and cafés, clothes shops and truck stops, salons and saloons, we decided the time was right for dinner.

Having picked our magnificent seven (there were actually five of them) to be the Politburo of this party, we decided on a treat to melt their hearts and their reservations: a dinner to remind them all of England far away. Joe had discovered a man he knew from Whitechapel working as a barman in the old oyster bar in Grand Central Station. And he knew that once upon a time, before his accident, this man, this Javeed, had been the very best in all of the teeming, torrid, Spitalfields district, the top chef in all Brick Lane. Straight, no chasers. And he agreed, with much pleasure and a little sadness at remembering his great triumphs, to prepare for us a mogul feast, the like of which the island of Manhattan had never seen. What true Englishman could resist?

And so we assembled: Little Anthony of the Barbarian Sex Bastards; Joe Kelly and myself; Fran and Toby, a hooray D J from Kensington way who had fled London to escape his parents' drug problems; Doreen Spooner, an artist and designer much hated by my beloved Rose, but much respected and with good reason; a strange little fellow called

Timothy, who had studied stage design at the Slade and recently opened to rave reviews with his dayglo, off-Broadway set for *Look Back in Anger*; and finally, Michael Smith, haunter of gay bars, philosopher, perverter of the young and probably the best barman outside the walled city of Kowloon. Michael at the age of thirty-four had reached a stage of grace and he knew everything.

The dinner was all saffrons and clay-reds, piping piquants and soothing raitas; all colours and all tastes, washed down with Kingfisher, king of beers. And, truth be told, so rare and captivating was this meal that we actually talked little. But then, after sufficient time for digestion we settled down to work. All present already had a vague idea of our plans, but we told them the whole truth of the future of England and of the party. And then we let them respond.

And the ideas that emerged were as follows: our launch party and presentation would be held at the British Boating Club, an arch waterfront bastion of the homeland, never frequented by the downtown trendies we were largely aiming at. We could secure this vaunted venue because Michael had had an affair with the manager of the place.

All chosen English folk throughout the world would receive an invitation plus the proverbial one. All others would have to try their hand on the door and plead to pay a paltry twenty dollars. This would make the local English particularly popular for a while, if nothing else.

We would attempt to secure a sponsorship deal from British drink companies that we had worked with before. That way we could at least offer certain free drinks.

We would erect some kind of stage and set, probably a street scene of old Soho. This, in particular, would teach new SoHo that it is not the centre of the world.

We would prepare a cryptic but tempting portfolio and presentation on Pleasure Inc. and England, using all the resources of video, tape, etc., that we could muster.

We would employ Javeed to prepare another fine meal for the chosen few allowed into our inner sanctum, 'An Englishman's Home'.

We would get the whole thing filmed (if not shown) by a local BBC stringer whom Joe knew.

We would allow it to be strongly rumoured (and, of course, denied) that the Barbarian Sex Bastards would be making only their second ever NY appearance.

We would give ourselves precisely one week.

And what a week it was.

Little Anthony actually sweated, diving into rehearsals with the band during the day, his phone book during the evening and clubs at night. Kelly and I seemed to spend most of our time in cabs, shouting at the traffic and the heat that made shirts stick to suits and suits stick to seats. The rest of the time was done deep in palavers, cajoling, cursing and caressing businessmen and suppliers, arty bastards and liars, hard men and hawks, promising the eárth and sometimes more, if necessary. We were lying and boasting and, above all, borrowing, for money was at a premium and most of it was Anthony's.

In the evenings we had to see and be seen, deny all rumours, fend off all inquiries and generally underplay to the maximum, so as to really wind the whole thing up. Michael Smith followed behind us, talking exact opposites and sowing the seeds of true confusion and excitement wherever he went. In the odd moments when I had time to think, I thought what a fellow he was; new to me, but obviously a kindred and kindled spirit. Finding a new one is still the greatest thrill. Just watching him work, his Englishness honed, his New-Yorkness complete. He was the perfect combination for this city, and he used it all like a master. If we hadn't found Michael, I don't know what we would have done. But then, you do find them, don't you?

And we soon found that it was working. Things can

happen in America, and our people made sure things happened in all the various New Yorks. Soon we were the talk of all the towns from gay to straight, theatrical to musical, fashion to finance, uptown to down.

And the local English responded as if the empire were at stake, offering help and advice and generally taking pride in taking part. And when, by Thursday, two days before the night, I felt confident enough, I phoned Gabriel and told him to get on a plane with an armload of London-life videos and his very best smile. For his charms, I believed, would now definitely be needed.

And as the time approached, the rumours that bounded back to us were remarkable. Lady Di was definitely coming. No one without a British passport would be allowed in. David Lean was filming it all. And I think it was a cab-driver who told me that the Beatles, or the Sex Pistols, were re-forming for the occasion. I think I believed him. I also thought that we had a lot to live up to. But it was surely too late to stop now.

We did have a few surprises in store. An Englishman called Ronald Wheaton, with a Vandyke beard, had made himself known to us. He had recently set up a business importing black cabs and red buses into New York as novelty items, and he was prepared to offer us free use of the entire fleet, plus drivers for the free publicity. Sade, the famous mulatto singer, who was an old, old mate from Boomtime days, happened to be in town and agreed to sing a duet with Little Anthony of a Chet Baker song they both loved. And Adam Coleman, the Brit Pack heart-throb, star of the hit movie, *Last Days of the Raj*, agreed to MC the event. He came from the same council estate as Diamond and was hot to do us a favour.

I didn't know what more we could do. I didn't really know any more.

It was one of those dog-hot New York days when your

clothes are wet before you put them on and the tempers rise with the vapours. It was one of those days when the whole city would take up claw-hammers and monkey-spanners to the heads of their neighbours if only they could find the energy. It didn't feel to me like a big day.

New York can turn on you like that. Suddenly the cockroaches and the cab-drivers, the madmen and the mountebanks gang up with that sapping, seeping heat to throw a switch which throws you from adoration to hatred. It just piles too high.

Home on 14th Street was also mounting up and beginning to look as though a siege had taken place, and I was faced with the dilemma of whether 'tis nobler to freeze in the deafening gale of the air-conditioning or melt in the homicidal heat. On top of all this I had a party to put on that could just decide our future. I cracked a can of Coke and looked around.

Joe was still sleeping on the futon, amid a pile of clothes, and I didn't have the heart to wake him. Kelly had worked. The last few days he'd been site foreman and press officer, driver, dealer and peace officer. His energy seemed endless but I could see that he was close to the edge. I guess my nerves were stretched too. I just wanted to get into a bed next to Rose and sleep . . .

I was tired, tired at that moment of these people with their easy, empty invitations and their tiny little worlds and their massive egos. I was tired of being in a city that neither knows nor cares about what is happening outside its walls, tired of their profound, childlike ignorance, their excitability, their lack of manners and their fucking intolerable heat. I was sure it would all come back tomorrow, but for now I didn't want to party with them. I wanted to punch a fair few of them and all their fat children.

Then the phone rang.

Now the phone rarely rang at 14th Street, because we'd

directed all begging calls through Anthony's record company, where a faggot called Caleb was acting as our secretary and loving every minute of it. So that meant it was one of us. But we, apart from me, should all be asleep. I'd gone home early because I couldn't handle any more. But the others had all been up all night. I wondered who it was.

I heard the hollow click of a long-distance call and waited. Then Gabriel's voice came on. He was supposed to have been on the first plane out of London that morning with an armload of propaganda and a journalist from the *Observer* who was eager for the story.

'Where the fuck are you?'

'I'm in Amsterdam.'

'What? Why?'

'Stop panicking. There's been a change of plan. We're coming a little later and we'll arrive there about eight o'clock. That gives us plenty of time. Don't worry, everything will be all right. I'm bringing a bugle with me.'

It's a real shame you can't throw long-distance punches. Gabriel was obviously pissed, and I could hear laughter in the background. I was just about to call him all the insults and tell him not to bother coming, when there was another click and he was gone.

I sat down and pushed the telly on. I felt like crying. It wasn't just Gabriel – he didn't matter that much. But once again we'd pushed ourselves into a situation where everything seemed to rest on one night, one bloody party; on the whims of a few hundred fashionables. Why couldn't I go home and trade currency or futures or something, make loads of money and forget all about morality? Live in Docklands and buy a Nakamichi cassette deck, vote Tory and not care like all the others? That is what I wondered.

I reached into my case, which was still sitting where I'd first left it, and pulled out a John Coltrane tape Rose had made for me. I fed the machine and waited for that sound to soothe me, to remind me that the world is good. Then the size and the warmth of that beautiful music, darker even than blue, began to flow over me and into me, with all its manly, melancholy understanding and all its humanity, and I thought of Rose. I'd barely thought of the girl since we'd left home. She was worrying me a bit, or rather I was worrying me, because I wasn't talking to her really any more, wasn't paying her the attention she deserved. I do love her, it's just that she's so strong and I've got so many things to do. I hope she understands; I'm not sure any more.

I picked up the phone and dialled London. It rang and it rang. Coltrane was playing 'After the Rain', and I thought of all she'd taught me and I just wanted to tell her. I felt calm now, but no reply came. Still, at least I tried.

'Come on, Tony, let's make this thing happen.' Joe Kelly was wearing nothing save a pair of boxer shorts, with boxers on, and smoking a cigarette. I put the phone down.

'Right.'

We met for a final lunch at a Japanese restaurant in the Village, which annoyed me by selling brown rice. There was me and Joe, Anthony, Michael and his boyfriend, Fran and Toby, and Tim. And instead of tonight, we talked of old times, and ate eagerly and earnestly, sushi and beer, and relaxed. Michael told us how pleased he was to have worked with us, how, since the end of the glorious times, when the sickness had come, he had felt jaded, felt saddened by all the deaths and the hatred. He told us how in the days of the Anvil and the Mineshaft and the Spike they had believed they were crusading for a better world, where pleasure and leather, pride and passion, lust and love and liberalism had all gone together in a riot of self-determination. He told us how he missed those days when the boys were in charge and a man could kiss a man. He wasn't just sad when he talked, he was proud.

I told them about Gabriel and all found it most funny, though I still could not see the humour in it. Then we discussed the few details that remained to be sorted and made a toast in sake 'to breaking legs and to great nights, to us, to England'.

I will admit the place did look good, all fitted and kitted out for perhaps the five hundred who would attend, might attend. And after a last check that all was in good order we retired home for an early evening of bathing and dressing, of shining shoes, folding handkerchiefs, of forgetting your worries by taking care in every detail, every inch. It was eight o'clock now, and we still hadn't heard from Gabriel. The party was set to begin at eleven sharp. At least I would look sharp.

Then, just as I was perfecting a windsor knot in the maroon tie chosen specially for the occasion and discussing an Orioles double play, the phone rang. It was 10.15.

Joe answered and I listened.

'About bloody time, too. No, don't worry.' He laughed his physical, shaking laugh. 'I'll dispatch something to get you. We've got just the job, you mad bastard. Good to hear you.'

He was grinning wildly as he turned to me. 'Gabriel's here.'

'I guessed that. What's so funny?'

'He's got a bit of a surprise for us. Don't worry, it's all fine, promise. I said I'd send one of the vehicles out to JFK to get them.'

'All right, but what's this surprise?'

'It wouldn't be a surprise if I told you, would it? Come on, let's go to a party. It's going to be good.'

And do you know? – I believed him.

As we pulled up together in a checker, through the silence of the riverside night, it all felt organized. After a week of rush and row there was an unusual, appealing calm hanging over the place. Michael was there, so was his team of urchins, all togged in the latest John Dullus Neo-Dickensian collection. The Dodgers and Olivers were barmen and gofers, and they looked perfect. The entrance was floodlit and chained. Fran was waiting inside drinking a vodka. Javeed was cooking in the back and Tony was spinning a selection of old hustles. The stage was hidden behind the Soho street scene, with the 'England' logo Doreen had designed. The portfolios, or manifestos, singing our praises sat on every table, and the band's equipment was all set. All seemed in order. The smell of Javeed's food hit delicately home, and I even felt that I could eat. It felt done, settled.

The first to arrive was Marina, a loud rake model from Tokyo, via Manchester, who was accompanied by a man who said he was in films. She apologized for being early, but said there was such a buzz that she wanted to be sure of getting in. She also asked me where she could get some ecstasy. I laughed and said I didn't know. That made me feel good.

Joe and I were to alternate on the door, along with Fran, who knew the city well, and Lou, Anthony's amiable bouncer, who was dressed, and I believe prepared, to kill. The cabs were picking up from a midtown bar called Witchcraft, for all those with invitations who wished to avail themselves. The first few people came by other means, and I wondered silently what had happened to our taxis; and to fucking Gabriel.

Then one of our cabs arrived, bearing a moderately famous graffiti artist, known, for some reason, as Mr Pillow. He was the hot art piece of the moment, which you could tell because he had his hat on back to front and four trash, art whores in tow. He came up to me, kissed me on the cheek and went to walk his entourage through. I asked for their invitations and he explained that they were with him. I explained that I didn't give a toss. And that as he had an invite he should pick the prettiest or the wealthiest and tell the others that he was sorry, but they could not come in. He was outraged. He told me that we couldn't do this to him, that Andy Warhol had been his best friend and that he could ruin us and our miserable party. Or words to that effect.

But just at that point Adam Coleman, our resident heart-throb stepped out of a cab with La Petite, a sixteen-year-old French beauty of much current repute. The flash-guns of a few waiting photographers fired, and I pulled them through.

Mr Pillow grabbed one of his troupe and shouted at the others, 'You can go walk. This is a private party.' And then he ran inside.

That was when I relaxed.

And those that followed him seemed to tally with almost every invite that was sent out. Add to that the few chancers who got Fran's miserly nod of absolute approval, and it was shaping up to be a fierce crowd. There were a few stars, but many more gems. Just the kind of tip-top professional crowd we'd hoped for. A few like Tony Newman, the *Vogue* photographer, and Jeny Daley, the model, had flown in from other bits of the world. Word had certainly spread, and it seemed, from talking to those present, that word was also well up on the England angle. But where was Gabriel?

It was now 11.45 and there was still no sign of our prodigal bastard brother. The show was due to commence at midnight, and he was carrying some important material. Joe, who still wouldn't tell me the secret of the surprise, didn't seem too bothered, so I didn't think I should be. But then, I know Gabriel.

Suddenly like some mythical beast of burden, a number nineteen bus came lumbering towards us, swaying a little and emanating a rumbustious roar that in one horrible moment I recognized. Oh, no. 'Here we go, here we go.'

Here they come. Gabriel leapt off, carrying an inebriate grin and a navy-blue Globetrotter, followed by maybe a score of my home town's most notorious designer hooligans, all of them very obviously pissed.

I didn't exactly conceal my displeasure. 'What in hell's name are you doing here?'

'Tony, your friends and my friends decided that a party is a party, so they should be there. We are the cavalry come to save the day.'

For a moment I really panicked, and I felt like telling them to fuck off. Everything inside was just fine, and I wasn't sure that it needed an injection of drunken desperadoes, showing that England might not be quite as sophisticated as we had been suggesting. Most of the rowdies were still painfully disembarking from the bus, so I pulled Gabriel to one side and asked him to tell me a story.

'Well, you know how it is when you do a foreign campaign. It all gets magnified back home. Your glory was such that this was the party of the year. So when they heard I was coming, this lot were all mad to go to England too. I couldn't say no, and besides, these are the best ice-breakers in the world. We ended up in Holland because the cheapest flight was with KLM via Amsterdam. And here we are. I told you we'd get here on time; in fact, we stopped at a few bars on the way from the airport.'

By this stage there was a huddle of baby Sloanes and hairdressers, a couple of clothes designers, a model or two, a minor-league pop star and an *Observer* journalist being sick on the sidewalk. Gabriel looked at me and looked hurt. He could tell I was not exactly overjoyed to see them. But then it hit home exactly what I was doing. He was right. These were my friends, and friends are friends, and a party is a party, after all. I looked into his dark eyes.

'Good to see you, Gabriel. Have a good night.'

And so indeed they did.

I can't say I did. I worked, drinking nothing but Rose's lime juice and talking little but politics. For I knew deep down that this was the reason we were here. I knew that night that we had to move it on, and fast, or else slide slowly into decadence. We had begun, I believe, with the knowledge that everything is there if you reach for it; and that you must reach for it if you can. But now a moment had arrived when we had to find out just how much there really was in us. Joe Kelly knew it too. In his different way he was just as serious as me. I realized then that there are two ways you can go. You can make the world small or you can stay in your own small world. I knew which way I wanted.

It was a good night, though; it had to be. The band was bloody marvellous. I hadn't seen them since before Paul's death and I'd forgotten what a true star Little Anthony is, all things good and all things evil; and I guess that's all there is. Except that when Sade walked on and sang 'You Don't Know What Love Is' in duet, there was more than there's ever been before. Impeccable.

And the whole feel of the party was one of well-cut efficiency of the highest order. It was a show and an advert and a time, and no one could fail to get the message and the intent. Gabriel's horse soldiers ran rowdily riot, climbing and falling and the like, but with such all-round good humour that they only added to the splendour. Outsiders, I hope, felt like they wanted to be a part; and some few said just that to me, that they wanted to be a part of England.

We had needed to gauge just how good an idea it was, and there seemed little doubt about that now. But we also needed to see if we could attract money. To be honest, we needed backing if we were to make England truly great. Come the end of the night I had a pocketful of promises posing as phone numbers. And a heart full of hope. I'd also had a stomach-full of fucking lime juice.

The next day was spent recovering. We'd hired professional cleaners, so we didn't have to do that. But we had to get ourselves into a condition to do business, and I was pretty close to exhausted. So I just stayed in bed all day. Joe crashed at the apartment of some girl he'd been seeing, to endure endless massage. Gabriel was told to enjoy himself because he was going back in two days. He was needed in London, and besides, I didn't see how his talents could help us right now. It was time to do business.

The situation as I saw it was this: Anthony was willing to invest fifteen grand as a silent partner (though he had no objection to us screaming his name). We could raise about ten grand from England, mainly as a second mortgage on the Pleasuredome. But we'd spent some on the party, so that left perhaps eight. I figured that with eighteen grand we could set up and start to run the agency. But I also now believed that we needed the shop straight away, to act as a focal point for England, a shop window, if you like. And to pay for a decent lease, decorate it and stock it would undoubtedly take a lot more than we had. There was also the question of staffing it all. Who was going to be Mr England in America? And who would work with him?

These were the questions that I turned over in my mind as I lay around the apartment. We'd come over here with an idea, but then ideas are cheap. Now that it was that close to coming off, the easiest thing would have been to bottle out, run away. I knew we couldn't. But I didn't know what to do next. So I slept.

The next morning I awoke to find a review of the party in the gossip column of *The New York Times* – good – and another in the *Village Voice* – grudgingly brilliant. There was also an answerphone full of messages, most of them from Kelly, who sounded excited. So I phoned Joe and he answered straight away.

'Tony. Good to see you're finally awake. This lunchtime

we've got a meeting that could mean everything. Last night at the Palace I met a Mr Rudolph Steiner. He's a businessman who's made many fortunes from numerous diverse activities, such as dry-cleaning and tin mining and the like, and he wants to give us money. He seems very sure about it all. He's a capitalist, and he wears Armani suits that are bought for him by a blonde girlfriend with big tits. But he's all right, seriously all right. I said we would go for a palaver at his towers today. He resides on 58th and 3rd, so come round here first at about twelve and we'll discuss it.'

I said yes, but I felt far from easy. We don't deal with people like that, they're the enemy. What about our independence? What about our principles? We could get eaten alive by something like this and end up in ill-fitting grey suits with company cars. It doesn't feel safe. I don't feel sure.

All of these thoughts were sitting uneasily in my mind as I went through the motions of a rather mechanical toilet. I had that ominous feeling of stepping on to a travolator, to you don't know where. And the strangest thing was that Joe sounded so sure. This was a boy who used to carry a copy of the *Daily Telegraph* in his back pocket so that he always knew what the enemy was doing. I wasn't at all sure that he knew what we were doing any more.

The phone rang again.

'Tony, good sir, how are we this fine morning?'

Michael Smith's wonderfully English voice came as a welcome relief from my thoughts of corporate America. I told him I was fine and he continued, 'A little something has come up which might be of interest to you. A friend of mine owns a space on Christopher Street. It used to be a bath-house, but sadly those days are long gone. He was at the party and he adores the idea of England, so he suggested to me that you use his space for your offices and shop. He hasn't really got any money, but he'd love to come in, and the building would act as his investment, so to speak.'

'Michael, God bless you. I do believe that you've just thrown me a lifeline. I've got to go to a meeting with Joe and some high-altitude businessman. But I think we might be very interested in you friend's offer. Phone you later.'

The idea of a little place in boys' town has a certain appeal, especially if it means we can avoid big business. That was the thought which I thought as I tied the laces of my shoes. I feel happy now, much easier. That's what I thought as I stepped out of the door and on to 14th Street. And as I walked up the street looking for a cab, New York felt good too, rather like home. You know where you are when you're at home.

Arriving at Joe's new home, I felt confident that he would be pleased about the offer from the Village. 'It means we won't have to deal with real America,' I told him. 'This is our world, Kelly,' I told him. 'I don't trust businessmen,' I told him.

'What the fuck do you think we are?' he said.

Walking into the entrance hall of Steiner's towers, I felt like we were entering the belly of the beast, being swallowed. His dominion stretched over the top ten floors of the skybound building, and we had to go to the topmost floor of them all to meet the man.

As we rode the lift high, Joe said nothing. But I could feel there was a tension between us. He was excited and I was disappointed that we had come to this. Or maybe I was scared. As the lift doors opened straight into a room complete with a girl and a carpet, Joe looked at me and smiled a serious smile before saying, 'Open your mind, mate, I think we need it now.'

Mr Rudolph Steiner, who met us with a handshake and a smile, was everything I expected: one of them. At a guess I'd say late forties, but fit and tanned, so he could be older and you wouldn't know. Receding and short, he was none the less possessed of an instant stature that even I could not fail to register. He looked at you and you knew he felt easy with the world, as easy, I think, as any man I've ever met. Like a man who's known demons, and fought them, and won. That is what I thought as I sat in that big polished office, with that dapper, polished man, who controlled, it was very obvious, many millions. Get ready for the life story, I thought. Here's a man who likes what he has done.

'Tell me about yourselves,' he said.

Now even distaste cannot stop me from telling a good story well. So between us, Kelly and I told him of the past and of the future, of adventures and successes. And all along we edited well and laid out plans that to me seemed sound indeed. We told of establishing an organization that would sell both the artifice and the artefacts of our proud nation. There would be an agency dealing in people and knowledge and a shop trading in things such as clothes and furniture, food, books, and braces; things, fine things. And there would be us, who, we could assure him, were the very best. And our team of expat experts promoting and advising and all round providing a good service.

And all along, in the telling, I was bolstered by the knowledge that none of what we were saying really mattered, because this was not our place. I knew that and I knew that downtown was where we belonged and would surely end up. But I was impressed by Mr Steiner, so I asked him why he'd asked us here.

And he told us, in his accent, not very different from that of the Brooklyn cabbies, that first and foremost it was because he had an eye for such things. He was, he said, a businessman whose business was making money; and money comes, he said, from good ideas. Dragged along to a party by his young girlfriend, whose photo sat upon his desk, he had seen a good idea well executed. And upon meeting Joseph in a discotheque had seen a man whom, he believed, he could work with.

He did, though, also add that he did not in fact need to make more money, for he was already wealthy beyond calculation. But he did need to enjoy himself, and he enjoyed helping others on ventures and adventures. He was, he warned us, a serious man. He had dry-cleaners and casinos and tin mines and the like. So we should not take him lightly, because lightly was never his way. He added that he was sure that there was a future in this England of ours, perhaps on a scale that we had not ourselves envisaged. And that providing, of course, all the details could be worked out amicably, we would be in a position to work together. What did we think?

Joe said we thought we would think about it and get back to him. I thought he was indeed an impressive man. But too big for us to live with. He bade us farewell and gave us two days to decide.

Riding back down towards earth in the elevator, I could see that Joe was well excited. I understood why, but I wasn't sure that he understood the full ramifications of all this. 'Let's go for a drink,' I suggested.

Sitting in an anonymous business bar, drinking a Long Island Iced Tea, Joe asked me what I thought, and I told him. He said that we couldn't keep hiding behind the walls of our little cottage industry. I said that we should go and see Michael's mate. I knew I had a fight on. I don't much like fighting my friends.

We rang Michael Smith and arranged to go straight down to the Village. He said he would meet us there with Ivan, the man who owned the place. It would take him half an hour, so we decided to walk. Up there, amid the midtown mayhem, I still felt a little jittery. We didn't talk much.

Joe was silent and serious. I was thinking about the meeting we'd just been through and what it meant for all of us. And all the while the streets rattled round my brains. As we got down past Gramercy and the buildings stopped reaching for the sky, I felt a bit easier, a bit more human. When we rounded St Mark's, and the punks were hanging out and there was music moving the street, I felt like we were back amongst our own. I felt strong and right again.

Then we hit the west Village and entered Christopher Street, and Joe Kelly grabbed me by the arm and spoke. 'Tony, the decision is yours to make. And whatever way you choose to go, you know I will back you. But remember what we came here for, and remember that we are good.'

'I know we are. And what's more, we are still on God's side. That's what I'm thinking about.'

Ivan, the minute we met him, was obviously nice people. He was a clone, but he had a sense of humour and he didn't seem to be a bad bitch. He was proud. And he told us how he'd run the place as the best bath-house in the whole west Village, before the sickness came. He hadn't known what to do with what was indeed a fine space, until Michael invited him to our party where he had had the best time in a long time. He loved London (he told us three times that he'd been there three times) and he loved our idea. He didn't really have any money, but he was willing to let us have the place rent-free, for as long as it took, and spend what he could on getting it together. What did we think?

Joe said we thought we would think about it and get back to him. I thought it was exactly what we wanted.

As we left the building, I expected a row with Joe. But he said nothing. I asked him what he was thinking.

'Come on, Tony, you know what I think: there's no comparison. But there's also no question of me trying to persuade you. I will support you, whatever. And I vow never to hold this decision against you, whatever way it goes.'

And with that he skipped off uptown, leaving me to stand alone in Manhattan and think. Melodramatic bastard.

It seemed fairly obvious to me. Although Steiner's offer

had all the money and the muscle behind it, that was not the family way. The place in the Village looked just about right; it was on a scale that we could handle, among people that we understood. I decided to phone Rose to discuss it with her as soon as I got in.

Rose was just going out when I rang. She sounded OK, but didn't really have time to talk things over. I outlined the problem quickly and she just said that I would make my own decision as I always do. Then she said she had to go. I told her I loved her. I'll be glad to get home.

That night I ate on my own at a little Ukrainian place up the road, drank some beer with the construction workers in the Dug Out, a dive-bar of fame just over the apartment, and I thought. Then before going to sleep I thought it all through once more, and one point kept coming back to me. It was that when we stood in Mr Rudolph Steiner's imperial palace, I thought, this is not my place, I know where my place is.

Then I slept.

The next morning I rose early and went to the local coffee shop for eggs and a read of *The Times*. Cuomo seems like a good man to me. Then I went back to the apartment and rang Joe Kelly.

'Kelly, it's Tony here. What time shall we meet Mr Steiner?'

You see, the thing is, you should never, ever know your place.

The decision made, we agreed that Joe would stay to take care of business, and for the time being it would be his base. He loved New York, and I think he'd also fallen in love with this girl Joanna that he'd been staying with. He seemed truly happy. We also phoned Mr Nathaniel Quick and told him to get over here as quickly as possible, because there was some serious business to be done. I had to get back to see my love. I feel there are better days ahead.

A Towel for Your Tears

Sometimes, I know now, she thought I never cared. I didn't ever never care, though sometimes, I now know, I didn't show just how very much she meant to me. Sometimes I loved her for ever and I always loved her. I know I still do. Rose and I are friends now. Friends is a funny thing to me.

At first, at first after the end, I mean, all I could really think is, I don't want to be lonely. I was just as selfish about that as I had been about everything else. But then after a while, and it had been a while now, you begin to miss the other person. My other person is currently a hole in my heart, a space where she once was; much more than a memory, more a hunger. But, as I say, we are still friends, fine friends, and that, I guess, is something, something we weren't for a while.

What seemed so strange to me at the time was that it should happen then, when everything else was starting to go so right. I know now that was just what she was waiting for, that's how good she is. At first, when I returned from America, she was cold, unexcited by our successes and my pleasures. But then, that next six months, when everything was happening so fast for England in the States, it was like wartime at home. There were long stretches of dull, difficult, dreamlike silence, punctuated by splintering, painful outbursts of violence, when one of us would lash out with an accusation or a demand. It wasn't like fighting before, because now we never really made up, never made it all right. We just started to fester.

She only punched me once; a roundhouse, farmboy punch, provoked by the accusation that she was having a lesbian affair with a girl called Irene (she wasn't). It landed right on my ear and hurt like fuck. It resulted in howls of pain and, after, a little laughter. That is the only laughter I remember from the bad time. The rest was tight-lipped, mean and bitter. It was a sad time.

But we knew there had been love, and there was still a powerful kind of something; so we kept holding on. I kept telling myself that we would come through, that this was a test that we had to pass, then everything would be better. We even tried to make love, using orgasm and closeness as some kind of panacea for our problems. It didn't work. But we never spoke of finishing. That was our taboo, as if once mentioned it would happen. And we couldn't really conceive of being apart. Or at least I couldn't.

And then she struck. It was the time of moving.

The flat in Wimpole Street was a dream, is a dream, the dream I've always cherished. But when it came to moving in, when the van was booked and the boxes full, when we were preparing to sleep in the shell of our last few years together, she spoke. 'I'm not going, Tony.'

I knew straight away what she meant, and that she meant it. The only thing I didn't know was how to respond. So I said, 'What do you mean?'

She looked sad and a little tired. Shaking her head slowly, she said, 'You must know, Tony. We both know it hasn't been right for a very long time; it hasn't been anything. Our love affair is over. I like you, you're a good person. You've been a fucking idiot. You've seen the world revolving around you and believed that was the only world. But I've always admired you, I still do. You've got a spirit, and the sad thing is you're getting better all the time. But our time has gone.'

Rose started to cry as she was speaking. I threw in a few

buts, but she just continued, with tears creeping slowly down her face. I remember now, she was holding a tea-towel, and for some reason I couldn't stop looking at it. She was wringing this piece of cloth, and I was in a dream again. But it was that hollow, hurting feeling of a bad dream in which your world is being wiped away from beneath your feet and you don't know how to stop falling.

'I've always respected what you've done, your friends and your ways, even when I hated them for taking you away from me. But you didn't repay that respect. You didn't just take me for granted, you took me for a fool. I know all about you, Tony.'

'But I love you.'

'I know that. I've always known that, which is why it has lasted so long. But you don't really know what love means.'

I tried to put my arms around her, tried to make it all better. I was crying too now, and we were both sticky with tears and heavy with the moment. Yet she refused to give in and relax into my arms. She didn't push me away; she just refused to relax, refused to let go.

'No, Tony. No, it's over. That's your problem. You think love is all about hugs and kisses when the darkness comes. Well, it's more than that, it's got to be.'

I was crying like a teenager now. Clenching my fists and wishing I could be a baby again, so that everything would go away, so that someone else would make it all better.

'But I can't live without you.'

'Don't be silly. You've lived without me for most of our time together. I kept telling myself you'd grow up; it's just come too late, that's all.'

'Rose, I promise I'll get better.'

'You probably will, Tony, you've got it in you. You've got fine things in you. But I need something else now, I need to live for me for a while, with someone who wants to share with me. Don't be sad, Tony. Don't make me sadder. You'll see.'

But all I could see was my future and my past saying they didn't want to be a part of me any more. My ground was gone, and I sobbed and I sobbed. And I think I cursed, or at least I wanted to. I asked if there was anyone else and felt bad for asking. I promised things, terrible and great things. And then after, I was all cried out. After all my emotions had been poured out in a tempest of sadness, when there was that large, silent, still time like after the rain, Rose went to the bathroom and brought me something.

'Here,' she said, 'is a towel for your tears. Cry no more, Tony, for now we are friends.'

Friends, as I say, is a strange thing to be when you have loved. It makes you think.

In those next few changing, moving days, when I pleaded and phoned, but knew deep, dark down that there was no point, I didn't really hope; but I did think.

I smiled when I thought of how we met. I cannot believe I was that person. But I hope I can find again a person as good and glad as the Rose I knew. She, to me, was like an English voice in a foreign land; like coming home when you don't even know you've been away. When I tracked her down to that plaster-showing, proudly peeling half a house in Kilburn and spent an evening talking (about me), I knew. Or at least I knew what I wanted, so badly. Yet I behaved all schoolboy noble and left with just a kiss (I know it seems silly after the way we met). Because I wanted it to be so right.

I can still sit and feel – not think – but feel what it was like; that tube ride back across London, that night when I first knew Rose. It was the same, my teenage mind told me then, as sitting down to an exam that you must pass, reading it and slowly realizing that you know all the answers. The paper you've worked and revised and hoped for has landed in front of you. You've still got to get it right, but you know you can. You're excited and you're serious, allowing yourself only a little smile, because you've got to plan your attack. You must not blow this one. But it is all there, everything you wanted, and more than you even knew you knew. That was what it felt like, that tube ride back across London, that night when I first met Rose.

Miss Rose was a foundling, though I doubt ever winsome, from Woking and was raised by two people whom she called Mum and Dad. A year and a little older than me, she was studying graphic design at the Central College of Art in Holborn and hanging out in gay bars, with boys in grey suits. But still I saw in her.

She had green eyes that turned grey when she was blue; dark, devil-dark hair, cut, when I first met her, in a severe bob. She had a face, brown, in the pale world of art, that spoke, to me at least, in volumes of strength; a wide, deep forehead, with eyes set down and far apart; a hooked, Arabic nose, which she always hated, and a round, but strong, jaw-line. She looked a little, I always thought, like a Red Indian. But then, that seems unlikely.

Her back was broad and muscular, like a swimmer's, and it tapered (though never as much as she would have liked), to a full waist and legs that were not long, but were perfect for the body they carried. She was a powerful beauty, though never one that screamed. And she carried herself like a warrior and a woman: upright, fluid and happy. She was noble and she was brave. And all of that is why I fell in love.

And indeed she had many followers. Boys had big eyes for Rose, and when she so desired, she had a big bed for them, if it pleased her to do so. I must admit, that in itself was part of the appeal; that knowing and that desire. But when I was finally welcomed into her house, it was a worry too. For I wanted her all to myself. And oh, how I wanted her.

We first made love the second time, the second time we

met back in London. After an evening of much drink and some rather hesitant fun in the bars of town, we returned together to her half a house. I felt nervous. But the desire that made me want to touch and feel and hold was stronger than anxiety, and I could feel that she possessed a desire all her own. It wasn't a heat, it was a will. And it came from far inside her body.

Her flesh was as smooth and strong and giving as I dared to remember. Offering and taking, opening and closing around me, in a profound conversation of skins. It became so that all I knew was her body, to be inside it, to devour it and to be devoured. It wasn't sex that was fun. It was sex that was very, very wonderful and good. And most of all, it was, and she was, more honest and open than any fine thing I'd ever known before.

And that first night, after our noises and our sweat, after our sex, when her head moved and her hips lifted and she slowly glided to a smile, she touched me on the lips and told me that she liked me, that maybe even she was enchanted. I told her that I was struggling not to say 'I love you.' And she looked, with her head held to the side and a smile, and said softly, 'Don't rush.'

But next morning, when we sat just talking, and this time she talked of herself, and her life, and I listened, I knew that this was a thing unlike; a strange and easy passion, strange and strong. I also resolved there, amid my joy and my desire, that this was a thing I would have to call my own.

The next few weeks were spent walking the tightrope of her love. Wanting to be with her all the time, yet not wanting to make her feel suffocated or scared. She seemed to me independence incarnate; wise and autumn cool. She was a girl, remember, like none I'd known, and I wasn't sure I knew how to get it right. Later she told me that she'd been charmed from the very first. But better indeed that I never knew.

Oh, Rose, I miss you.

I miss, of course, the sex. Those times early on, three times before lunch, when we drowned in our sex. A sex so sweet and thick that it stuck to us and made us smell. It was a sex that, even in the bruised and bitter times, was never less than good. Sure, I miss it now it's gone. But not as much as I miss you.

Then there were the times, the swaggering, sniggering, drunken times, such as when we stormed castles and threw sand and lay down and failed to make love on the top of trucks parked in the street. And we tripped together and we travelled. Do you remember, we ate snow and we danced and used such language as only we could understand? For truly then we felt like spies, me and my best mate, who was equal to and better than all the greats I'd ever known.

I miss too, and I always will, your talent. It was you, Rose, who showed me that creativity – that witchcraft which dangled mystically over us all. You taught me that it's an everyday, an all-the-time, but never an ordinary, thing. It was you who taught me to stop being easily impressed, but to be deeply impressed by easy talent. It was you, and I remember the day, in that chic and spruce and dense half a house in Kilburn, which holds such memories, who taught me to hear John Coltrane.

You taught me that day a little history, of bebop and berets and the like. Then, without flinching, threw me straight into that rounded, awkward, giant of a man, with nagging, spiteful teeth, who sat for a year in his room alone, throwing off the tiger on his back and thinking. Then he emerged, to paint the most profound and challenging sounds we have ever heard. On the Impulse label he played. Dancing and daring us to follow his path, through all cultures and all emotions, talking *Giant Steps* in three and four and five tongues, all fluently and all at the same time. Those bitter, burning, beautiful vocabularies that John Coltrane blew: you taught me.

After that and for ever, we swapped love stories, like Dylan Thomas and Knut Hamsun, George Sorrell, Marinetti and Marvin Gaye, Picasso and Spencer, Gerard Manley Hopkins, Federico García Lorca, Agatha Christie and Ben Gazara, Prez and Billie, H.G. Wells, Nash, Gaudí, Smokey Robinson, Robert E. Lee, George Jackson and W. Eugene Smith. It was always a certain sadness to me that you would never share in Johnny Haynes and Georgie Best, Babe Ruth and Garfield Sobers and the others. But then I sort of understood that we had to have private worlds too. Though in that first, evening-filled year, we seemed to live together almost always.

When, after a few months of my not asking, you finally told me to move in that night when I discovered a gun, I swore to myself that I would do this well. But I thought 'well' meant washing up, making good love, and listening to John Coltrane together. I wasn't so good, I don't think, at listening to you. You see, I always saw you as the strength and the understanding; you understood me, so obviously the world was all right. It was fine because we looked good together. It was fine because I could make you laugh and because you smiled every night when I kissed you and told you to sleep with the angels, like they do in Spain. At first we always went to bed together.

I think the reason I didn't give you more was because you never asked. I know that sounds like an excuse, but I was stupid. Sure, you'd shout, and we'd fight, but that always seemed to me a sign of just how close we were. Even when I was spending less and less time with you, and our lives sometimes met, rather than really being one, well, that just seemed the way it was bound to be. It's funny how you don't notice things changing when they are a part of you. Or at least I didn't.

Of course, I know now how much and how often I took you for granted. You were Rose who was there. Rose who was fine. Rose who was quietly being a big success. We could still have those moments, when I wanted to squeeze and scream because there was so much love. But at one point I guess it was squeezing out the last drops, screaming for a memory. And when you aren't laughing as often or lusting as often, you tell yourself, well, that is the way of the world. And we all learn to accept the world as it is.

We still had good times. Dancing. That thrill of being with you in a room where all were looking, of feeling how good you moved, how close in rhythm we were, of looking as you danced and still seeing love in you, never went away. Maybe it was only an echo, but it was love, no doubt, whenever we were dancing. But dancing should never have been enough.

Not even holidays should have sufficed. Like in Paris, when we walked rivers, and fought cab-drivers, and sat and watched, and were just like lovers. Or that time in Rhodes when we expected an idyll and found ourselves living in a disco full of sunburnt swingers. Again we became a conspiracy and a team, as we laughed at all and everyone and revelled in our drunken superiority. And why not? We were good together, always. It's just that we were truly together less and less, and I let that happen, made that happen.

I even told myself it was fine when I started seeing other girls, said that the occasional spot of infidelity keeps you faithful, that it was OK as long as I remained loyal. Whatever that means. I saw another girl in the first week we were together. It seems odd now, now that I would give up everything to have you back. But she served only to tell me how different and how important you were. So I told you. You threatened to kill me that night, and my heart soared that you cared so much and sank that it might really be the end. I never told you again.

Though there was nothing to hide for nearly two years. I was so involved with you then, what now seems so long ago, that I got jealous of your dreams. I would lie and look at you sleeping and wonder who was making your eyelids move, who was making you turn. I wanted to wake you a few times to demand to know who you were dreaming of. But I never did.

I remember the first time you left me. It was to go to Berlin. I felt as if a piece of my body had just walked out of the door. It was physical, like a limb was gone. No, not a limb, but some vital internal organ that had been wrenched out, leaving a gaping, wanting emptiness. That's how I feel all the time now. It's sad how we don't fight to keep those feelings, how we just let them fade away. Five years is a long time fading.

I could not have grown up without you. But I suppose I used you as a support rather than a partner. I hope, above all, that I gave to you too. I know once, in our dark ages, you said that you got nothing from me. But I cannot believe that you really meant that. I hope I taught you lightness and laughter. I hope I gave you hope and the belief that you could be seriously and easily happy, even if I couldn't actually make you happy. I hope also that I showed you the crack and how powerful and right it is. And I trust that that knowledge will live with you, as you live now in me. For there was a magic about us both that should stay with you as a beacon for ever. It still burns deep in me.

And now that we are friends . . . Now that I sit in airports and think of you, and talk to you, even though you are somewhere else, with someone else . . . I hope you are happy with him (on my bad days I still hate him, but never truly, because you have chosen him, so he must be good), and I hope that you think of me as happiness; and I pray you wish me well. I am a boy of twenty-five and I love you. And if I ever fall in love again it will be for you and because of you.

'*JAL flight twenty-six is now boarding, gate thirty-six.*'

In Which the Unsteady Crew Enters to Remind Our Hero that Fun, After All, is Fun

I saw a man at the airport with a funny face and it made me laugh. But it didn't last long. Seventy-five quid for a stuttering, faltering cab ride through a city that looks like LA with a hangover is not likely to make many men happy. I'm not sure about Tokyo. I know I haven't seen it yet, but that's not everything. There's something about the idea of it that I don't like. Though I'm willing to be proved wrong. That's why I've come here three days early.

I like hotels, though. If I'm with somebody else, I like old hotels, full of character and characters and cornices and wrought iron and stone floors and mysterious rooms with no apparent purpose. But when I'm alone, I like the introverted anonymity of four modern stars, where there's nothing to do but switch on the television, run a bath and think about yourself. There's something wickedly, wilfully selfish about being in one of those bland, faultless hotels; a conspiracy of one, wallowing in melancholy without sadness and watching pictures that you don't understand in a room you don't care about. I know, I'm in one now, and I could happily stay here for ever, raiding the mini-bar and reading the menu, if only it didn't make me feel so guilty. I think, when I'm old, I'll live in a hotel. Only now I'm young and I ought to see the city. Six o'clock is always a good time to see a city.

That comforting, romantic anonymity that you get from modern hotels goes for towns too. There's little as lovely as walking alone through a new town, where you know nobody, where there are no demands or debts, no favours asked, no memories. There's plenty to see, but nobody really sees you, you don't register; just another foreigner in a foreign town. On the road in from the airport, Tokyo didn't look very foreign, but it certainly feels it. It feels upside-down.

America standing on its head is what Tokyo feels like when you start to walk aimlessly around its clean, polite, scrambled streets. At the same time it's more western than the West and more eastern than I'd ever imagined. It is full of concrete contradictions, anachronisms in action, as something old and something new sit side by side, turning a blind eye to each other. They don't compete, they co-exist in confusion.

See what I mean? 'Joint Jeans Living', proudly boasts the neon on the department store selling 'traditional' cookies that bear the legend 'With All the Goodness of Your Mother's Bosom. For a Winning Life and a Healthy Retirement.' This well-stocked, shell-shocked shop also boasts an alarm clock that will automatically readjust to local time anywhere in the world and a palm-sized photocopier for the modern spy. I cannot make myself understood, so I do not buy anything. Not buying anything in Tokyo feels somehow illicit. Still, perhaps foreigners are exempt from the rules. The rules seem very important here.

The business I am on, here in Tokyo, is fairly predictable. It is to oversee the opening of the second branch of England Overseas. A year and a bit after the inauguration of England, New York, and its immediate, modestly massive success, the opportunity to go oriental has presented itself. Mr Rudolph Steiner received a phone call and made two, and the whole thing was just about done. Joe abdicated the chance of leaving his Manhattan home. Jimmy and Gabriel deal mainly with Pleasure Inc., so here I am. The only problem is, I haven't got a clue where I am, or where the President Hotel is from here. Time for another cab.

Dining on sushi and beer is just dandy. Watching the fat man with the sharp knife perform delicate, but never dainty, operations on uncooked fish in the time-honoured way is almost as much of a treat as the food itself. Today it is tuna, salmon, conch and eel.

There are in this world a few fine things that deserve their reputations: good red wine, strawberries, smoked salmon, oysters and truffles, linen, cashmere, fine stationery and raw fish. All these things are to be indulged in sparingly and with a due sense of awe. I hope Tokyo doesn't make me blasé about raw fish. I'm rather bored with being blasé. Tonight I shall go out.

The reason for going to a club in your home town is that you know who will be there and you want to see them. When you are alone and abroad, it is entirely the opposite. You can talk to strangers in discos in strange lands. Or you can choose not to talk at all. Both options have a definite appeal. So do the machines in hotel corridors that shine your shoes. A man feels like a real person when his shoes are shining.

Of course, before you go anywhere, you do a bit of homework, and I had a small list of low-life highspots. It was already a little late for a bar, so I opted for a club called Tokyo. A club called Tokyo seemed somehow apt, like diving in head first. According to the map in my room, it wasn't very far away. But I didn't trust myself walking round the warren at night. So I got the hotel reception to call a cab and tell them where I was going. I'd been warned that Japanese cab-drivers don't like picking up foreigners at night. It seems to me they don't much like foreigners.

But I was quite excited at the idea of being a foreigner, intrigued to see what strange delights a Japanese disco would offer. We pulled up in a strangely silent neon-bright side-street. I paid a king's ransom for the cab and prepared to find out.

There were a couple of young Japanese girls standing by the doorway as I walked up, and they giggled self-consciously when I smiled at them. I'd already decided that it would be easier to pay than go through the ritual 'can pay, won't pay' in Japanese, when the man behind the desk motioned me to walk straight through.

'You no pay,' he said sternly, as if I were somehow insulting him by offering.

Ours is not to reason why, I thought, putting my money back in my pocket. Then I realized what music was coming from inside. It was 'I Love Money' by Little Anthony and the Sex Bastards. I couldn't believe it. You come all this way and they play a record by your best mate. I wonder how the Japanese dance to that, I thought, as I pulled open the heavy sound-proofed door and stepped into the dense, expectant darkness of the club. I walked a few hesitant steps while my eyes adjusted to the lack of light. Suddenly I heard: 'Tony.' I think I actually jumped. When I returned to ground, there was six solid feet of smiling beauty, with outstretched arms to greet me. Polly Stanford, cover girl, friend and a long-time fancy, was standing in front of me looking like a peach.

'Tony, what are you doing here?'

'I thought I was being alone on business in Tokyo.'

'You're hardly alone. Jemmy's here, and Gayle and Dee – I think you met her in New York. Oh, and Susie Parsons is here, but she's not out tonight. This club is specially for models. The agencies all pay for it. It's shit, but you'll probably know half the people here. The Americans are disgusting, but everything's free, so we all come. Come and have a drink.'

Looking around, I could see that we were in a small, rather tacky seventies-style disco, where almost everybody was tall and tanned and decidedly occidental. There were a few frail Japanese girls doting on the boys, who were doting on each other. There was also a handful of somewhat shady-looking Japanese men in their best John Travolta gear. Everyone else was obviously a model. Many of them were obviously rough American models, and a couple of them were dancing rather perfunctorily on the tables. I couldn't help chuckling. Welcome home, I thought.

Sitting at the table with Polly were half a dozen English girls, all but two of whom I knew. They all seemed genuinely pleased to see me. Especially Polly.

Polly is made up of a series of long brown lines, topped by a waist-length mane of ginger hair. Loose-limbed and languid, she walks like a cat, which, I guess, is why they pay her vast fortunes for doing precisely that along the catwalks of the various fashion capitals. She is vaguely celebrated in the wafer-thin world of fashion trash, but always gained my respect by laughing off their laurels. She has a strong south London accent and a strong constitution, for she takes far too many drugs and rides on far too many aeroplanes; as they all do. But she still manages to look very beautiful, in a rather obvious model way. She is not what I expected tonight. But quite what I could do with.

'Tony, tell me everything.'

Sitting closer to me than could really be justified, Miss Stanford seemed excited and happy, in an open, defenceless way, which I had quite forgotten existed. Her ease was contagious, and I began to talk the tales of London Town that she longed to hear as only exiles do.

I told her of the great Soho riot and how it had ended, with a man in a skirt being pursued by four policemen at five in the morning. I also filled her in on the details of the 'agency and the ecstasy' scandal that was currently rocking model-land. I told her, though she already knew, about Dangerous Jane and Danny Marney getting married by the sea. And I told her, too, about me and Rose, and she seemed sad, though not completely. She told me that England in

New York was the best shop she'd ever been in and that the boots she was wearing were from that very source.

It was then, I think, though I cannot be sure, that she ran her hand over my thigh. Then she asked me if I'd seen Shinjuku yet.

I told her that I didn't even know what it was. She laughed and said, 'It's all the movies you've never seen. Let's go now.' With that she grabbed my hand, jumped up, shouted a goodbye to the others and pulled me to the door with the half-skipping, half-loping step she employs.

As we went outside, I was aware of a rush of excitement at feeling that her hand was still in mine. So without giving myself time to think about it, I pulled her round and kissed her on the mouth, a mouth that became soft as soon as it registered what was happening. I remember thinking, that's the first time you've kissed anybody since Rose left. But I didn't dwell on it. She responded by putting her arms around me and continuing the kiss. To me we felt like equals.

After a few seconds we broke for air, and she beamed a big, happy smile. I winked. We squeezed each other's hands. The funny thing was, neither of us said a word. Instead she hailed a cab straight away and climbed in, still clutching my hand. Maybe they lied to me about the cabs.

Shinjuku wasn't so much like a movie as a moving, living, video arcade, where you are both the player and the game. Polly knew her way round the neon maze like an expert, steering us from delight to delight, colour to colour, pointing out the sights and the sounds in this place that buzzes and beams and burns aloud. Here were teenage *yakuza* with their tattoos and their transvestite gangster chic. Here were businessmen who'd drunk too much whisky from their own personal bottles, lying in their suits in the street. Here was a machine that transported you to planets, here another that made you a baseball star and a third that predicted accurately your future in five languages. Here was the screen upon which *Blade Runner* was so famously based, and here a bar where you could get your willy out. And at such times, when stopping at traffic lights or in front of curiosities, she kissed me or I kissed her. And both of us howled and squealed at the foreign things we saw. Yet I will admit that I found some parts sad. Though I was considerably happy in myself.

And at points we stopped to drink: swift, steaming sakes and at one place an Absolut vodka, which we slammed, to the considerable merriment of the indigenous population. Yet, more intoxication came from the cacophony of the places than from any alcohol. Just when I was becoming tired and thinking warmly of bed, the lights of Shinjuku began to blink and the sounds stopped. Then, and I promise you this is true, a tramp in a doorway, with all his sprawling entourage of bags and bits, prepared for his night's sleep by taking out an alarm clock from one of his many pockets, setting it to the appointed hour and placing it by his bedraggled head. Indeed this seemed to us like a sign. It also seemed to me a deeply melancholy thing. But Polly is impervious to such sadnesses, she lives off only fun. Tonight I was to live with her.

We were both tall when we walked into the foyer of the President Hotel, and the sleepily admiring glances of the night man followed us into the lift. There we snogged for the few computerized seconds it took to travel to the fourteenth floor. We were both feeling, I am sure, that special combination of friendship and lust which is such a different experience from love. It is a clean feeling and quite a rare one, when it involves no complications. This night for me it was the best feeling in the world. This night I also felt that maybe I wasn't a bad person.

In the morning we sat and ate the breakfast we had ordered by telephone, and shared the time we had together.

Polly was possessed of a body which was a dream to wake up next to. Especially when you knew that a few hours earlier you had been a part of it. Just sitting on that hotel bed, eating toast and watching her walk, was a real pleasure. She knew no embarrassments and stretched the long brown lines around the room with the grace and ease of a photograph.

Knowing that I could reach out and touch her at any time, and be met with a purr, made me feel good. At that moment, on that morning, she was the best friend I could ask for. For she asked for nothing and gave warmth and laughter.

Later that day she had to fly to Milan to wear some clothes; another plane, another dollar. I had business to do in Japan. We had had a fine time, and now we knew that rare luxury of having no plans together. We had no idea when we would see each other again, and it didn't matter at all. I was twenty-five, nearly twenty-six, and beginning, I believe, to see the light again, to remember how brightly it burns. We kissed each other when she left and she even turned round and smiled.

I travelled to the ancient temple at Asakusa, riding the underground railway alone, bolstered by the closeness I had recently known. Here I saw schoolgirls dressed as sailors and a monk with a bald head and a tin begging plate. And outside the temple itself I followed the ancient ritual of those parts by leaning over a fire in a well, bathing in the sacred smoke and there making a wish. I wished hard and actually believed that now it might come true.

Later that evening I met a man called Gene Karel from Philadelphia, who was recommended to us by the venerable Michael Smith as somebody very special. Michael was not wrong. Forty-two years of age, he had hair like a river and ideas like a pirate. He spoke nine languages, including Japanese and Swedish, and for some reason kept cracking jokes about Dom De Luise and Edgar Lustgarten. He laughed his way through a pile of sushi, delivered to our plate by conveyor belt, and into a job for which, not being English, he had few qualifications. I can only say that in the next few days Gene Karel was to save my sanity.

It was fucking horrible. Maybe it was me, maybe I just didn't understand. But I have never in all my life had to deal with so many manners and so few morals. I have never been misled so consistently, nor been faced with such inefficiency and such fear, and this from people who are supposed to know best. That was my experience of business in Japan.

The simplest tasks were smothered in layers of etiquette and hierarchy. The simplest questions were invariably received with a web of contradictions, which always began with the word yes and ended up with me no wiser. Nothing was straight, and nothing, I'm sorry, seemed honest. I was treated throughout with the utmost politeness and the minimum decency. Of course, I expected problems dealing across two such different cultures, but I never expected to be treated like a barbarian by people who will bow to you but show you no warmth. Gene, for reasons that I cannot understand, actually likes these people, and saved me a few times from swinging at them and for them. And these were meant to be the ones on our side.

If that, as they say, is to be the way of the future, then I am a sad man. For it seems to me to be a future of feudalism and racism, sexism and cant. In fact, it looked to me like all the things that were wrong with the past; plus computers. In the end we had an agency and a shop in Ropongi, which were roughly like the ones we wanted. But don't ever ask me to go and visit them. I had a heavy heart and a sixteen-hour journey home.

On that journey I slept in snatches, drank in quantity and thought. I thought that business is not a bad thing, though the people involved in it have many lessons to learn. Business is just a machine, but at times the machine can wear you away, and it becomes a thing then that is not pretty. Money too, I guess, is fine. Far better, Heaven knows, than poverty, which holds no pleasures and few mysteries. But sometimes money actually gets in the way. It makes so many demands upon you.

All these things were tumbling over in my mind and getting a little tangled. What worried me most was how quickly and how far I'd fallen after Polly had picked me up. I wasn't sure exactly what was going to sustain the highs any more. At thirty thousand feet on the journey home, I felt a little low, felt jaded and battered and ready for sleep. I didn't really know what I needed. Although I was sure I needed England. Cry God for England.

I always try to travel light. And I'm pretty good at getting to the head of queues, so it wasn't long before I was off the carousel and out through Customs into Jerusalem. I would soon be able to crawl into my own bed and sleep and sleep. I felt like sleeping a lot. I didn't really feel like very much else. And then I saw the Unsteady Crew.

Meeting people in unlikely places is becoming something of a habit with me. But then, you sort of expect to see the Unsteady Crew at airports. Airports, bars and sports stadiums. The members of the Unsteady Crew take their pleasures.

There were five of them on duty, and they were Tommy Moore, the Creature, Bobby, Squirrel and Steve, gathered in a misshapen huddle of abused designer clothes just outside the automatic doors to the airport. I couldn't tell if they were coming or going, but then, to be honest, they don't usually know either. I wasn't sure if I wanted to risk talking to them; these, you must understand, are dangerous people, and I'm a tired boy. But no matter what, I will not be rude. These are my friends.

'Hello, Squirrel, what's happening?'

The Unsteady Crew is always pleased to see you.

'Dad, what are you doing here?' he said, after kissing me on both cheeks.

'I'm going home. Hello, Creature, Tommy, Bob, Steve.'

I continued my greetings and Squirrel continued talking: 'No, dad, don't be silly. You're coming to Barcelona with us. Why else would you be at the airport?'

'As it happens, I'm just on the way back from Tokyo.'

'Exactly, and just in time, too. The plane doesn't leave for an hour yet.'

'Leave me out, Squirrel. I'm not going to Barcelona. I've been travelling for sixteen hours.'

'So what difference will another couple make?'

'I'm tired, mate.'

'You can sleep when we get there. The match isn't until to-morrow.'

'Oh, no. What match?'

'Barcelona–Real Madrid, of course. An extremely important game, I am sure you will agree. Steven here knows a fellow with a large safe house that we are welcome to, and he can also get us tickets for the game, so we're off. Come on, get the plastic out and buy a ticket, you wastrel.'

'I can't really. I've got things to do in London.'

He looked amazed. 'What sort of things?'

'Business.'

Squirrel stared at me as if I'd just fouled the footpath and turned to go. At the last moment, though, he turned again to look at me with hurt eyes. 'All right, dad, but you disappoint me. I never took you for a spoil-sport. I really believed you were after the crack.'

What could I do? Next thing I knew I'd phoned Kelly to tell him I was taking a little break, and I was back on a plane in the company of five smiling street arabs, planning plunder and talking sport.

Now, this Unsteady Crew, this world-famous obscene

team, is a group of men. They are also desperadoes and outlaws; one at least is respectable, one is rich, one is dodgy and one is a gambler. Together, though, they become the warriors of the way of life. These are men with a mission: to boldly go where they went the night before, and stay there until forcibly ejected. They like sport, mostly, and parties. And they are without any rudeness.

Life for the Unsteady Boys consists of consumption and camaraderie, and they are truly full of charm and laughter and not inconsiderable intellect. Even they, however, would admit that they are more than faintly ridiculous. It is just that they have made a conscious decision to milk this existence for all that it can offer and to offer fun in return for all those who cross their path. They ask little, save all there is, and are very willing to travel to get it. You must never, though, ask them where the money comes from. Just watch where it goes.

And going with them on this plane, on the way to this famed Spanish place, I was told with all their usual enthusiasm that Barcelona is a city of cool splendours and big fun, and that a few days there would do us all the world of good. They also stressed that the Camp Nou Stadium full of *aficionados* is a sight that all true lovers of spectacle should witness.

I am sure that is true, I thought, as my excitement grew. Of course, I was still tired, but these boys with their open, smiling charms were rapidly lifting me. Just being in their company was making me considerably happy. It's funny how happiness is all in your head.

And besides, I thought, I've got some people to see.

But even the worst-laid plans of men can go wrong. And, of course, they did.

When we arrived in the blue of Barcelona, the answerphone of Steve's man informed us in two languages that he was away for the weekend in Ibiza. No flat, no tickets.

These boys, though, are far too unsteady to panic. So we piled into taxis and straight to a hotel that our Steve highly recommended. Tickets for the game would be procured outside the ground.

'There is nothing in the world that we cannot get into,' said Tommy Moore.

'What would life be like without adventures?' said Squirrel.

These boys, you see, are like that.

On the ride in from the airport, Barcelona looked pretty unremarkable. Then we entered the old town, drove past a couple of squares, down a dense and dark side-street and to the Hotel Novel. It was all the things a cheap hotel should be: it was cheap. Actually, it was beautiful in a sort of gracious, tumbledown manner, and after arriving there with my friends on a sunny Saturday afternoon in search of sport, it didn't seem to matter that the water in my shower was cold, the towel torn and the telephone purely ornamental. It wasn't even a matter of any great tragedy that I had no clean clothes whatsoever. This trip was certainly proving to be an education.

It was decided that once settled in, we would go out. To wander, then to eat. The Barcelona that we walked into was a rumbustious, almost oriental place called the Ramblas. This street, with its cascades of flowers and birds, bootblacks and European news-stands with the news of the world upon them, was something of a market. It was also a promenade, which we paraded and sampled and took great fun from, until such time as it was decided that we should eat.

Now Steve, who had adopted the mantle of tour operator, claimed to know a fine Catalan restaurant covered in tiles, deep in the district known as the Barrio Chinö, a mysterious Chinatown with no Chinese. So we followed him through a fascinating, but unfathomable, maze of medieval alleys and back-doubles, across courtyards and through squares, past transvestite whores and *gitano* encampments, until he finally admitted that even he was lost and we must ask.

So, amid many English giggles, our embarrassed leader used his rasping cassette-course Spanish to ask the way of a man who I swear was a smack dealer. And with great charity this man led us through the warren for a few minutes and actually led us right to the door. It was shut.

Instead we settled for beer and *tapas* in a bar like every other. I ate squid and Russian salad, fried potatoes with a kind of chilli mayonnaise, anchovies and cockles, and finished with a vanilla ice-cream in a plastic tub. No one was unhappy. But no one mentioned that we might not get tickets for the game tomorrow, though I know we all thought it. I went to a machine and drew some money on my card. Spending money, I thought, is a good thing. I was just hoping that I got the chance.

Having eaten, we decided to drink a few glasses of the local, dark-red wine before going back to the Hotel Novel to change into night attire and head for the local heavens. The last thing that I remember was lying on my bed for just a few moments to take a little rest. When I awoke it was to-morrow.

It transpires that my friends had smiled gently on me when the time had come to go a-raving. Realizing that I was genuinely exhausted and not just suffering from cowardice, they had shown me considerable kindness and had allowed me to sleep. They, of course, had done little of that, but lots of everything else. This they told me over a breakfast of beer and sandwiches. We also talked excitedly of football. A big game is a very big thing.

The cab took us as far as it could, before we got lodged in a morass of traffic, solid with the excitement of the impending event. Anyone who follows footballing lore knows that this contest is way up there. It felt like we were walking to a wedding or a war.

I knew most of the history; of Cataluña versus Castile, of these two great cities, represented by collections of men who have meant more than just football. And football, I knew, meant more in this country than most anywhere else. As we approached, and I could see now that the great stadium we were walking to was on the same scale as this history, I knew that it was all well worth it. I was excited.

We got tickets easily. Getting them was almost an anti-climax. We were so wound up about the prospect of having to hunt and hustle for tickets from a Spanish spiv that it came as quite a let-down to find that we could just walk up to the box office, give them the money and go in. There weren't many tickets left, and we probably had the worst four in a house of 120,000. But we had them and, as they say, it's being there that matters.

And even high up in the heavens of that vast cauldron, you could feel just how much it mattered. This was a place for partisans. When the two teams walked out into the sun, I felt a little sad that I wasn't really a part of it. I was going to enjoy this game, but I wasn't going to live it. My stomach wasn't aching. I didn't find it difficult to sit still because of the tensions. I uttered no prayers.

I also felt sad at that moment for Fulham. I hadn't been going to see them lately, and nor had many other people. So I vowed there and then that I would make a real effort next season. Fulham and football are too good to lose. But who do I want to win today? Looking down at the two teams, I suddenly switched allegiance and opted for the men in the regal white of Real. I am twenty-five years of age, I thought: and I've still got a thing about men in white shirts.

Out in the shining sun on the green field, a slow game of technical mastery and occasional quicksilver brilliance ended in a two–one victory for the Catalans, with much rejoicing by the north. To my mind, though, a young man called Emilio Butragueno, who is known as the Vulture and moves like an eagle, a man who sports the all-white of Madrid, was the star. He scored no goals, but won a place deep in my memory. The turn of his body and the speed and width of his mind made everything worth while. It is good to know you've seen, with your own eyes, some good things in this life.

'Shall we go to a club tonight?' said Tommy Moore.

'Certainly,' said Squirrel and Steve.

'No,' said I. 'I'm going to see my sister.' Or, at least, I hoped I was. I guess I was being a bit presumptuous, expecting my sister to be in when I called, after three years of not visiting. But in she was. And true to form, she didn't sound in the least surprised when I said I was coming round. Just pleased.

131 Calle Aribau is a typical old Barcelonan block of flats, with wrought-iron railed balconies, shuttered windows, patterned stone floors, high ceilings and cool light rooms. 1a, 131 Calle Aribau, also has a walled terrace, where you can sit amid the bougainvillaeas and take the sun. There was no sun at nine o'clock on the Sunday evening when I arrived; just three people I liked a lot and a bottle of 1964 Rioja, opened specially for the occasion. We sat on the terrace, though.

Maria, Fred and Xavier had been to the beach and had got home only just before I called. I had seen them all when they'd visited London, but I had never seen them looking as good as this. With the sun burnt on their own faces and in their own city, in their own home, they looked like people in the place they ought to be; looked exactly like I've never really felt. They all smiled and they all kissed me, and we were pleased to be together.

Xavier is somewhere in his mid-thirties and is a charming, gentle, straight-backed fellow, with a square jaw and a square, uncomplicated nature. Fred is eight years old and five parts Spanish now; an urchin, but a well-mannered one, who speaks English with a Spanish accent and Spanish with an English one. He calls me Uncle Antonio. Maria is a grown-up. She's put on a little weight, but it looks good, and a tan definitely suits her. Maybe it's the Latin in us, but she seemed to fit in perfectly here, more than she ever did in London. The pace is right, the priorities too, and there's a church opposite, so she can carry on where our mother left off. I wonder sometimes why I'm so un-Catholic.

After Fred had climbed over things, and under things, and showed me his toys, and chatted away in excited bilingual tones for an hour or so, he was put to bed. It was then that Xavier got out the wine, and we sat in the still of the night, without even music, and talked.

They wanted to know all about my adventures, so I told them. Sometimes you feel embarrassed, flash, saying what you've done and where you've been, but they genuinely like to hear it, for, I think, they genuinely like me. Maria knew all about Rose, because I'd written and told her and also because she natters all the time to my mum. She was good about it, though – the best. She said it was sad, but better that we split up if things were bad. She also said that I should learn from it and grow up a little. I told her I thought I was.

Xavier is great. He doesn't speak that much, but when he does, it's always firm and sure and sound. He's got hairy arms and he wears a gold watch with a metal strap. He is manly in a way I'll never know how, and he loves my sister. He told me they were in the process of buying a house in Menorca, and trying with no success for a second child. Maria told me Barcelona was a good town with much to offer and said she would take a few days off work to show me round, providing it was all right with her boss. Her boss smiled and said he'd think about it. I didn't even mind when they behaved like a couple.

They offered me a spare room to sleep in, but I declined and said I'd see them in the morning. On the way back I thought of trying to find the boys in a club, but decided against it on the grounds that I might succeed. I also thought that I did not envy my sister's way, but I did understand it. That in itself is quite an advance.

In the next few days I was shown a city with a stature and a style all its own. A big, gracious, seaside city, where people sit and talk and play in the mountains, and stay up late, and go to the Picasso Museum, and work, but never too hard. The city was at the same time both baroque and balanced, cool and passionate, and as easy as anywhere to be in. With seas on one side and mountains on the other, it was a kind of valley of visions, of mad modernist follies and clean modern sweeps of wide avenues; it had trees and many newspaper stands and alleyways. All the time and everywhere I wore only shirt-sleeves, which was such a treat.

I learned while I was there to eat Carpaccio, which is not Spanish at all but Italian, and to drink Carajillo, which is a local speciality of small, dark amounts of coffee and liqueurs of aniseed, often taken for breakfast. It is sweet and strong, like the people. I also learned the secret of the Sacred Family, what a *tertulia* is, how to windsurf and how to take little boys to the zoo all on your own and live to tell the tale.

At night, only once did I rave with the Unsteady. It was, though, a long and fruitful one, continuing way into *mañana*. My comrades had ensconsed themselves far into the local scene and over the days had recruited the assistance of a couple of redoubtable members of the local nightclub Maquis.

So together we wound a riotous route through the night, which led us into designer bars and out of them again, into discos and clubs and parties and eventually, as the sun rose, on to a tram and then a funicular, which carried us up a mountain towards a Jesus and a fun-fair. And sitting, cans in hand, on this mountain called Tibidabo, we rested.

There, as we watched the city and the sea beneath us, we talked of many things. Among our conversations was one concerning the dearth of an adequate ideology for the times, which set me seriously thinking. Another and most enjoyable one centred on just which are the top five nightclubs in all the known world. After much well-informed debate, the list we finally compiled was this one:

Westworld, London
The Wag Club, London
The Garage, New York
Save the Robots, New York
P. Einz, Munich
Otto Zutz, Barcelona

And then, at the very end, after we had talked ourselves all out and the city was busy, the sun was hot and we were quiet, Squirrel, who thinks a lot, even though he is a drinking man, turned to me and said, 'Do you know, Tony, friendship is good?'

I told him I did know, and he was pleased about that. Then we said farewell.

I thought about many things in that time in Barcelona. 'The Rose of Fire', they called her during the Civil War. Then her wild sons and daughters, such as the famed Buenaventura Durruti, spat and sang their anarchies, proud and deadly in the faces of the fat and ugly Falangists.

And you can still feel anarchism in the air and in the people. Walking her streets, sitting in her *bodegas* and her bars, watching her sea and her mountains, I began to think that anarchism, that bold idea, has a place in a world where the factories and the shipyards and the production lines are dismantled or manned only by machines. Man can once again regain his place at the centre of his own world and stand proud and individual. High-tech anarchy is certainly something to take into account, I thought. A serious thing for the times.

I met others in Spain, including a strangerman who showed me considerable kindness and an English who had a good tale to tell. And I fell not a little in love with that country and her funny, conservative, radical ways. But mostly in that week of mostly sunny days by the sea, I fell in love with my family, and we talked together a lot.

Maria told me that she was proud of me. I didn't really understand. Proud of what, I asked. She said she saw in me now a far better person than the one she'd envisaged, say, ten years before. I was an arrogant little bastard then and now I wasn't a bastard at all. She said she thought I was actually a little example of how to get by in these times, which for me was going too far. She also said that she was sure that I would get exactly what I was looking for. I told her I didn't know what I was looking for. She smiled and said, 'Tony, I will teach you a Spanish word as a present, a word for you. And your word is *duende*.'

Of course I said, 'Thank you', but felt obliged to ask her what it meant. We were pissed, which, I guess, is why she forgot to tell me.

'Oh, yes. *Duende* means elf or imp. And if people ask me what my brother is like, I shall say, "*tiene duende*". He has a certain magic. Like Johnny Haynes.'

What a wonderful gift.

To little Fred I gave gifts too, such as a precise knowledge of the rules of cricket, a tin of English toffees, a Barca shirt, a side of ham, a book of Tintin, a brief run-down on our family history, a gun, a knowledge of Paul Diamond and a transfer for his arm. Then one day out on the sunny terrace, amid the bougainvillaeas before he went to bed, he asked me to tell him a story. And the story I told him was one that I had heard myself.

The Story of the Big Man and the Brilliant Goal

It was sunny – I was in Spain – when I heard this story, told to me by a big man in a small bar, and the story was, he swore, in all parts true. It concerned the same man, but was set in a different time and place, when he was younger and far smaller and living in a port full of the bustle of all nations. There were Indians, Greeks and Magyars, who fished the seas and then, when finished fishing, played football, in all their languages, with the boys of this busy, big seaside town.

Now, this boy who liked to play football with the Sikhs and the Orthodox and the atheists also had a strange love for the lean, but manly, beauty of the electric bass guitar with four strings; he played it from the age of thirteen, strapped high on his chest, and cleaned it with a cloth kept specially for that purpose. This was considered a strangeness in this heavy, northern, working town, but still a girl fell in love with him and, as was the way, agreed to be engaged.

But one thing she could not agree to was his following the talent in his fingers and making his guitar sing. For she feared that this would impair their chances of a nice house and happiness in the heavy town. So even though he was good and growing, with a reputation as a budding bassman, he kept his instrument locked in its case for almost all of two whole years. Instead he had reasonable sex with the girl and went to Scamps, and Bailey's, and Romeo and Juliet's, where they occasionally fought in the way that young lovers do. They also saved in a joint account for the day soon and sure to come when they would marry.

Through the auspices of his father he secured a position as an apprentice to the trade of boiler-making, which he did well and with some satisfaction. Occasionally, such as when he saw a pair of brown high-waisted A-line flares, price eighteen pounds, in Arthur's, a shop of no mean repute, and she threatened to leave if he bought them, he doubted the beauty of their arrangement and wondered about his future. But in the heavy towns in those times there was a real poverty. Not the poverty of depression and recessions, which was yet to decimate this dockland, but a sapping, draining poverty of expectation. So he expected nothing more.

But still he followed the Tigers. On Saturdays and sometimes midweek under floodlights, he thrilled to the manly, yet cavalier and at times exquisite, skills of the local heroes, who wore golden shirts. Football was a thing of beauty and pride, and the likes of Simpkin and Chiltern and, above all, the godlike Wagstaff could create those moments which burnt into his soul and remained animated there for ever. This was fine by the girl, though she did not share his love; for football, after all, was something that all young men liked.

Then one fine Saturday, an important day indeed, for this was the Football Association Challenge Cup, the Tigers were drawn to meet Sunderland FC, a team which proudly wore the red-and-white stripes of their heavy northern industrial town. This team contained such luminaries as Jim Montgomery, Pop Robson and Dave Watson, a gargantuan, raven-haired man who wore the cap of England in the position of central defender and terrified lesser men. Sunderland was a big team, a very great team, and it carried the hopes of many young men and was expected to win. This game meant a lot to a lot of people; to our boy it meant, at that moment, most everything.

Now in the forward line in the golden shirt that day was John Hawley, a curious man who held no legally binding contracts and retained, even in this age, the status of an amateur. He also played football of a light-hearted, though powerful, nature; he was a big broad man, with a sense of honest style that endeared him to many. It was expected that up against the international skills of the gargantuan Watson, he would have little chance to shine. All the followers of the Tigers, though, hoped against hope.

And when he scored in the first half with a simple tap into the net, the hearts of the home boys soared. And then, in the second, a thing of wonder occurred. With his back to the goal and Mr Watson in close and menacing attendance, the amateur Hawley received a long-flighted ball, just inside the Sunderland half. Controlling this ball, but maintaining its momentum, Hawley drove towards the goal, all the while being pushed out to the byline by the gargantuan Dave Watson. Then suddenly, as he reached the edge of the penalty area, still facing in the wrong direction the amateur Hawley knocked the ball up, pivoted, swivelled and volleyed it straight into the top right-hand corner of the goal. Watson, for all his England caps, could do no more than stare.

Our boy, though, knew he had seen a thing of magnificence, a thing that would remain with him and excite him and inspire him for as long as he could cherish the exploits of big men. Then, when John Hawley executed the mystical, magical hat trick of footballing mythology by climbing over the rapidly diminishing Watson to head the leather home and see the Tigers to victory, joy and wonder were complete.

But, upon returning on that great and good Saturday to the company of the girlfriend, he was dismayed to see that she mocked and belittled what he had seen; that she poured scorn and dampness upon his burning pleasure. Not only could she not share his excitement, she seemed to think that it was wrong, unnatural to know such romance and such aesthetics when you are apprenticed to be a boiler-maker in a heavy working town and are currently saving to be married. This was, it seemed to her, a dangerous delusion, like playing the bass guitar. He could never be a musician and the Tigers could never win the Football Association Cup.

Now, truth be told, the Tigers never did go on to run round Wembley Stadium, with their golden stockings rolled to the ankles, receiving the accolades as they held the silver trophy high. And John Hawley finally signed professional forms and lived out his career as a good, but never glorious, jobbing footballer. But in the argument that ensued that evening in Scamps or Bailey's or Romeo and Juliet's, the engagement was cancelled and the ring returned and the boy, still only seventeen years of age, finally found himself free.

The next week he also found that he was free of half a joint bank account, which had been swiftly emptied by his erstwhile fiancée. But still, he had his bass guitar with four strings. And I guess you've guessed that he went on to know considerable fame and fortune as a master of rhythm, reaching even as far as Spain and further, and in the process becoming a big and gentle man and being all-round considerably happy. She married a man who turns off the television every time our hero plays bass in the corner of their living-room in the little house in the heavy industrial town. Where no one, not even the Sikhs and the Greeks, plays football on the docks any more.

A Philosophical Discourse on the Body Oikos

'We must begin, it seems obvious now, with a new way of distributing money. A way which relies not on work but upon the knowledge that work is a thing, for most, of the past. And thank God for that.'

I said that one lunchtime in a restaurant in Fitzrovia that I don't normally visit and I didn't expect anything to become of it. I often say things like that. But then I haven't said anything remotely like that to Joseph Kelly for a very long time, because he hasn't been here. But here he is, eating English food as a special treat. A starter of home-made oxtail soup with sherry is enough to fortify anybody, so I thought I might as well throw it in. What with it being nearly Christmas and all.

'Yes, I agree, but it is not enough to rely on old Marxist mantras, about each according to his need. Stalinist *noblesse oblige* is no answer. We are in real danger of returning to a kind of serfdom of service, where the working rich keep the non-working masses, as retainers. Bureaucratic socialism has no answer to that.'

Joe was looking serious and sipping from the very un-English Bordeaux. He looked well. For someone who'd been in New York for eighteen months, he looked unbelievably well. I could see that he felt like a big talk, so I continued, 'Definitely. The individual must be paramount in any attempt to think out the next phase. It all points in that direction. Industrialism created collectivism, because it was the only defence mechanism that the working classes had. The sick thing now is that in Britain we still have the class system, but we don't have any workers any more. We have entered a post-industrial age, have no doubt about that. We were the first industrialized nation and we are the first to go beyond it. The individual is out there on his own again. But how do we reconcile that with a collective conscience and a belief in equality of opportunity? I still have those.'

The main courses were just arriving, and I was quite impressed by the service. Vivaldi was playing in the background when the man brought my game pie and Joe's beef cooked in Guinness. It was actually cooked a little more than he would have liked. But it didn't destroy his concentration.

'I don't know, Tony. To be honest, I can't really think of a way of reconciling the two, but I know it is going to have to be extreme. For me, it has got to contain elements of old Communism. I still believe in the collective ownership of wealth at its source. But I can also see that individualism is much more logical now, and in many ways more revolutionary. Most people aren't working in factories any more. It is all smaller groups, or individual enterprise. Most of the kids we team up with are pirates now. If I think about it, I don't know a single person with an actual job, not one. And I'm sorry, but I believe that's a good thing. I don't think that work has any intrinsic value, and I don't see why people should work at all in the future if they don't want to. For some people, maybe many people, not working is going to be their role; and as a society we've got to provide for that. Or else we accept a massive, permanent pauper class and an aristocracy of those in work. That is everything I despise.'

'Me too, but that is precisely what's happening. I've been thinking about it a lot and I've come up with a set of ideas that, for want of a better name, I've called social hedonism.'

My comrade in the dark-grey Gaultier suit and the ginger

hair laughed a little laugh. 'That sounds to me like the way we are.'

'It is. What I've done is to try to make sense of the way that we've lived our lives, and make some kind of coherent economic theory out of that. I know it's vain, but you know what I'm like, and anyway it's funny. But it's also serious. Somebody's got to think about it. The Left certainly aren't. They are still fighting for a return to wage slavery for all, which is both stupid and wrong. I think we should be trying to eradicate work as much as possible.'

'Yes, but it's got to be replaced by something.'

I cut in quickly. 'It's got to be replaced by pleasure. That sounds a bit hippy, but we've got to start educating everybody to enjoy their lives, to achieve their maximum potential as people, rather than training them as factory fodder for jobs which no longer exist. It's about altering the whole basis of society.'

'But, Tony, nobody can maximize their pleasure or their potential if they are struggling just to live.'

'I agree, and that is where the social element of social hedonism comes in. We must institute a social wage, whereby everybody in Britain gets given a certain amount of money per week simply because they exist. The state already pays out loads of money in the form of mortgage relief, unemployment benefit, child benefit, old-age pensions, etc. But we do it all wrong. At the moment, the more you earn, the more you get back. Yet if you are really poor, the minute you start to earn a little money, they stop your benefit. For me, the social wage has got to be inviolate. It must be paid to every citizen and it must be enough, so that if you don't want to work, or you cannot find work, you can live comfortably.'

We were nearing the end of the meal now, and we'd finished the wine. My pie had been good, though I thought the vegetables, particularly the parsnips, were a little soft. I ordered some French asparagus, while Kelly had a bread-and-butter pudding. We both had coffee and cognac. It was Joe who picked up the conversation.

'That sounds OK as far as it goes, but it isn't that radical. In effect it's just a juggling of the figures of the welfare system, which has failed for so long to bring about any real changes. There's got to be a much more profound assault upon the ownership of wealth in this country.'

'Of course there has. Look, let me explain a couple of ideas. They're a bit mad, but to me they make sense. At one end I think we've got to totally liberalize all trade. As far as I am concerned, the individual must be able to make money and spend it in whatever way he or she chooses. In that sense I am a complete libertarian, and if somebody wants to buy or sell sex or drugs, start up a television station or sell the Bible on a Sunday afternoon, that is up to them. In fact, they should be encouraged to. Any society needs the energy and the enterprise that comes from individual endeavour.'

'You're beginning to sound like Thatcher there.'

'Shut up. I'm sounding like an anarchist, and I think that's very important. And I go further. I believe wholeheartedly in zero income tax. I do not think the state should take away any of the money you earn for as long as you live.'

'Well, then, how do you pay for the social aspects? I can see the hedonism for a few that would result from that, but it is hardly redistributing anything.'

'Wait. There would be a tax on everything you spend, and since everything is legal, you would bring the black economy into the system. But much more importantly than that, there would be no provision in this system for any kind of inheritance. Absolutely everything would pass to the state when you died.'

'That is radical.'

'Thank you, Joe. The idea is that while you are alive, you can earn whatever you can and spend whatever you like.

But equality of opportunity, and sufficient resources for social expenditure are both ensured by absolute death duties. So, in fact, all wealth is commonly owned, but you can take back as much as you can while you are here. And it goes further. All land and property would be owned communally too, but it would then be leased out, so that if you can afford it, you can rent Buckingham Palace for an astronomical fee; or a council flat for next to nothing.'

I finished off my brandy and continued, 'This system of state property rental would ensure another source of revenue, to be spent on the social wage, and also provide the widest possible choice, while eradicating the iniquity of inherited land, which is still at the heart of our class system. The whole idea is to create a system which is fundamentally hedonist, rather than materialist. But with equal opportunity of access to pleasure.'

'Gentlemen, I am afraid the restaurant is closing now.'

We argued a little over who was going to pay, but Joe's new gold card outbid my ordinary one, and so I let him get it.

'Shall we go to my club?' I asked.

'Why not?'

I had recently joined a dining and drinking club in old Soho, which allows a young gentleman to buy a drink throughout the day, a perfect example of enterprise in action. We walked across the tawdry clamour of Oxford Street and down into bad-town continuing our economic discussion. Joe threw in a couple of objections, which I tried to answer.

One obvious one was that you could not allow money to be siphoned out of the country and sent abroad. There would have to be quite a rigid authoritarian aspect to the system to ensure that it was fairly operated. As we crossed Soho Square, and a light, reluctant snowfall began, I took up that point.

'I'm a libertarian, not a liberal, and there would have to

be a rigid implementation of the rules to stop the desire for dynasty building. But I actually think that Britain, under this system, would be an attractive place for people with a large earning capacity, because we wouldn't take any of it away from them in taxes for as long as they lived. Someone like Little Anthony who is now in tax exile, would be straight back. Obviously, if you then want to travel, you could take out certain amounts, but we certainly could not allow anyone to take the advantages without contributing at the end.'

'It feels bloody good to be home,' said Joe as we entered Dean Street.

I signed us into the club, gave our coats to the girl behind the desk, and settled into a settee for a drink. Joe said to me that he agreed with a lot of what I had said, but that I hadn't addressed the central issue of work and its role in the future. I was hoping he would say that.

'As I said earlier, we have to begin with the viewpoint that most work, for most people, is not a very pleasant, fulfilling or even desirable thing. Work isn't horrible, as Marx believed, because workers are alienated from their labour by capitalism, but because they've got shitty jobs. I don't see any way in which anybody can gain satisfaction from putting biscuits in boxes, or assembling cars, or going down drains. They do it solely for the money. So if we can make machines that do those jobs for nothing and continue to make the same profits, then we can pay those people for doing nothing. That is where the social wage comes in. Obviously, it would require the complete nationalization and mechanization of all large-scale industries but I take that for granted.'

We ordered a good bottle of Rioja from the cellars. I must admit, I've been very taken by Spanish wines ever since my visit and now drink little else.

I continued with my theory. 'I also believe that, although

leisure is a form of liberation, most people would not choose to do nothing. They would use some of their time to supplement their social wage by whatever means they could, trading in whatever skills they possessed and keeping all the money they could make. Or else they would just sit around and drink and talk and go to the movies, and what is wrong with that?'

'Nothing whatsoever, I agree. But machines can never totally replace people, and there will always be unsavoury jobs that need to be done, both in terms of creating wealth and of maintaining our society . . .'

'Of course, and I've thought of that too.'

'I thought you might have done. Tell me.'

'All right, if you insist. Seeing as work of that kind is recognized as something unpleasant and demeaning, then why not make it a punishment? At the moment we have a prison population which costs us fortunes to keep and which contributes nothing. Why not, instead of locking people up and letting them rot expensively away, make them do the jobs that need to be done, for no payment? So instead of being sentenced to prison, you would be sentenced to work down the mines, down the drains or in the factories.'

'You can't have mass murderers walking the streets, even if they are mending them.'

'I know that. And I am afraid that, for crimes like murder and rape, I am in favour of the death penalty. There is no place for people like that in our society, and no point in paying all that money to keep them outside it. I accept, though, that there would have to be provision for confining some few people too dangerous to be set to work, but not many. I also believe that crime will decline due to the social wage, to the decriminalization of drugs, etc., and to the fact that pleasure will replace property as the inviolate principle in our society. But there will always be people who have a debt to repay, and they could be put to work.' I felt quite pleased with myself at that point and raised my glass in a silent toast while I awaited his next question.

'Do you really believe that would provide a sufficient work-force for everything that needs to be done?'

'I don't know – we would have to see – but I have got another idea if it doesn't. If we needed more workers for those jobs which are not deemed to be intrinsically reward-ing, then there would be a system of conscription; national service, if you like, whereby for a set number of years people could be set to work for the community, as they used to be to fight for it. But don't forget, the whole aim is to minimize the amount of monotonous work that has to be done, by maximizing the use of technology, in order to make people unemployed. Then people can use their time to better effect, for greater pleasure and profit.'

We were both maybe more than a little drunk by this time, and questions and answers were taking a little longer. Along with the sips of wine.

Joe thought for a few seconds before speaking. 'OK, I accept that, and I realize that large-scale manufacturing in-dustry is not likely to play much of a part in Britain's future. We are being Canute-like in trying to preserve and create non-existent jobs. But we are still going to need skilled wor-kers and wealth creators.'

'They aren't even affected by this. The wealth creators in an entrepreneurial sense can be even more effective, because they are not tied down by any kind of trade restrictions or faced with the disincentive of income tax. They have every opportunity and encouragement to become multi-millionaires and fully enjoy their wealth. Skilled workers can sell their skills on the open market, or else work for the large state-run industries for competitive rates. But I do think that in the future skills will become more personalized and individual again as large-scale manufacturing declines. We will see a return to artisan skills.'

I stopped for another drink. I was improvising now, and it wasn't that easy with a mind that was a little damp. I took a deep breath and continued. 'The only restriction on enterprise would be that any business over a certain size would pass to the state as soon as their founders died; along, of course, with all their money. After all, you cannot enjoy your wealth after you're dead, can you? There's no door charge at the clubs in heaven. And obviously your offspring can't have it, as that is iniquitous. It's a very meritocratic system this.'

'But what about the likes of teachers and nurses and people whose skills cannot be traded on the markets? Where do they fit in ?' Joe was slumped pretty low in his seat now and clutching his glass tight. I thought about nurses for a couple of seconds before answering.

'Of course, all health care and education would be provided by the state, and anybody who worked in those areas would be very well paid indeed, so that they would not need to look outside the state system for money. It would have to be illegal for any private education system to exist, because of our absolute dedication to the principle of equality of opportunity. But education would be a massive growth area, because whole-scale, encouraged unemployment means that education would become a lifelong process, as you continually educate yourself for pleasure. Private health simply shouldn't be necessary. The state that genuinely owns all its wealth would be a rich paymaster and provider.'

Just at that moment a young gentleman called Barry, who used to be a thief in Dalston and now directs adverts, walked into the club with a bad Ebony suit on his back and a bad page-three girl on his arm.

'Good afternoon, boys, what manner of skulduggery are you up to this afternoon?' he said in his best manicured market-trader voice.

'We're having a philosophical discourse on the body *oikos*,' said Kelly.

'Oh, right,' said Barry. 'Fancy a drink?'

'Cheers. Two large brandies,' I said, and turned back to Joe. 'The central point of it all is that the social wage must replace work as the mechanism of maintaining the majority of society in the essentials. Then enterprise can replace work as the mechanism for creating wealth. And pleasure must replace wealth as the barometer of success. Work should ideally be banished to a barbaric past.'

At that point two brandies were delivered to our table by a black-haired, Italian waiter called George, who is studying law in London. We both took a sip and thanked our benefactor, who was now in deep conversation with the girl, who obviously had a great future in advertising.

I was really rocking now, so I just wiped the foam from my mouth and continued. 'The moribund proletariat must be superseded by a new non-working class, enlightened on the joys of pleasure and leisure and energized to the possibilities of their own piratical potential. We must wipe away the clinging bourgeois morality of conforming corporatism and replace it with a society powered by individual liberty and protected by communal care. We must move, full speed, to a future of fun and freedom for all, and that can only be achieved by the adoption of the system of social hedonism.'

I picked up my glass and drained it with a flourish, banging it down on the table and falling down into the chesterfield.

'What do you think?' I said.

'I think you drink too much,' Joe said.

Another Day Older

I think I'll go into work today anyway.

The walk from my flat in Wimpole Street to the offices in Wardour Street is rarely a difficult one. The city glides past in a nicely mechanical muse, offering few unwanted surprises, save for the occasional jackhammer or siren.

Today it is at its calmest. It is that early-spring London, where everybody is so surprised to see the sun that they smile; and maybe even wish you good day.

Soho is not what it was, though, and it saddens me sometimes to see the changes. It's gone from jazz town to media village. It used to be hard, and you could get drunk round here. Now you daren't step out of line for fear of being reported. Soho's not what it was because there's too much money there now. Sometimes I wonder if I'm not what I was for the same reason.

Still, I will not allow myself to be unhappy. I have come, after much consideration, to the conclusion that unhappiness is a condition of extreme vanity. I am twenty-seven years of age. Today.

'Hello, Tony. Happy birthday.'

'Cheers, Margaret. Another year older and deeper in doubt. What have I got to do on this good day?'

Sometimes it seems silly me having a secretary, but it would be bloody silly if I didn't; nothing whatsoever would get done. I threw my Filofax away when they appeared in the *Sunday Express* magazine. I always forgot to look at it anyway. Margaret never lets me forget anything. She is wonderfully good at her job. She came from a nightclub and she cares. She also taps the desk with her left hand while she talks.

'I've written out a list of calls that have come in. There's not too much – a query or two from Japan and a request for an interview from *Interview*. There's also some accounts to go over, but they can wait. Don't forget, though, you've got a lunch with Alan Porter.'

'Who?'

She looked at me with her fiercest telling-off face. 'Alan Porter, the film man who Mr Steiner was so anxious for you to meet. I've arranged for him to arrive at your club at 1.30, and I thought you could stroll round from there to that new place, Smith's, in Greek Street, which you said you wanted to try. They don't take bookings at lunchtimes, but I'm sure you'll be OK.'

'Thanks. What do we know about this bloke, Margaret?'

She was smiling now. 'Well, obviously you don't know very much. I know that he's a millionaire producer who started out in London during the sixties, producing swinging pictures for pop stars with pretensions to cinema superstardom. Nowadays he lives mainly in California and makes movies and millions from the poolside, I suppose.'

Margaret always talks like me when she fancies taking the piss a little. Her grin showed that she thought she'd done it rather well. I was less happy.

'Just what I fancy on my birthday: a fat lunch with some bad-taste, Californian arse-hole with a gilt complex. The things I do for England.'

'It might not be that bad; he could offer to make you a star,' she laughed.

I turned to walk into my office, but Margaret asked me one more question that made me turn round: 'What would you really like to do on your birthday?'

'I'd like to meet all my friends at once.'

Walking into the high-tech facsimile of 221B Baker Street that passed as my office, I felt guilty for a second. Maybe I should have told her that line came from a disco song. Still, even if I didn't invent it, I certainly meant it. I would really like to see my mates, all of them, and to see them all well. I think that would be a perfect day. A bit self-centred I know, but better by far than California scheming.

I spent the rest of the morning dipping my toe into telephone calls and newspapers. I didn't feel like immersing myself in anything. At 1.15 I decided to wander round the corner for a meet and lunch.

'Don't forget, Jimmy and Gabriel are coming round to your flat for a drink early this evening,' said Margaret as I left the office.

Too much money and too little sex. That's what's happened to Soho. They haven't so much cleaned it up as washed all the colour away. The neighbourhood has been drained of almost everything that made it interesting. It has been whitewashed in the name of wholesome homogenization. They have converted a tenderloin into a series of high-rent rendezvous for the communication classes. And the worst thing is, I'm a part of that. Some answers you just can't know. Although you can think about it. You can think about a lot of things walking three little streets east. Funny how birthdays make you reflective.

Walking past Ronnie Scott's, I saw from the hoarding that Chet Baker was due to appear the following week and made a mental note to go and stand with my left arm on the bar and listen. Chet Baker never gave in. But then his teeth fell out, and he resides full-time in cockroach motels. That, I am afraid, is no answer either.

I reached the club.

Parked outside was a car.

Now, since I moved into Wimpole Street, I've dispensed with the use of a motor car; it never seemed worth all the attendant grief. But this was a car. An immaculate late-fifties black Citroën D S. Decapitable, like the one de Gaulle drove, with a soft white hood, drawn down in honour of the early sun, white-leather bench seat, hooded lamps and a body longer and sleeker even than Polly Stanford's. This, I thought to myself, is the kind of car they don't make any more, because they daren't.

'Do you like the car?'

I swivelled to the voice behind me and blurted something out in schoolboy embarrassment. I felt as if I might have tarnished it just by staring. 'I'm sorry, I was only looking.'

Watching me was a thin man of indeterminate, but roughly middle, age. His hair was perhaps a little longer than it should have been, and he was wearing a nicely tailored navy-blue suit, deep in the Savile Row tradition. He owned a tan that was fresh golden, but not vulgar. And, looking down at his feet, I saw a pair of black beef-roll loafers, worn with black socks, which instantly dated him *circa* '64. He also had a nice face.

'There's no need to be sorry. I'd be gutted if nobody looked at it.'

I don't normally talk to strangers, but I liked this fellow, so I continued the conversation. 'It's wonderful. What year is it?'

'It's a 1958, but, believe it or not, I'm actually only the second owner. I bought it in 1968 when everyone else was selling their cars to walk to India or somewhere. I got it cheap.'

I swear he had love in his eyes as he stroked and praised his beauty. And you could tell from its immaculate condition that this machine had been cherished. It was nice giving him compliments, because you could see how much he enjoyed them. He was like the boy who got the train set. And I was in no rush to deny him his joy.

'It's in wonderful condition. It must be worth a fortune now.'

He was sitting on the side of the car, not posing, just proud. 'Well, it certainly wouldn't be cheap, but then you could get three of these for the price of a Porsche, if you could find them. Most people with money just haven't got the taste; they want status things, not fine things. There's another advantage to this car, though – they can't clamp it, because of the hydraulics. It is the perfect nonconformist's car.'

He was very happy now and talking like we'd known each other for years. I was just nodding and enjoying. He continued, almost without breathing, 'What do you know about this club? It must be new. There used to be a really good little Italian here in the old days. I've got to meet somebody here, and it's all changed. It's a while since I've really been in Soho, and I don't recognize it.'

'I was just thinking that myself. Where have you been, then?'

He looked almost embarrassed as he answered, 'Los Angeles.'

I gave a little chuckle.

'Don't laugh, it's not that bad there.'

'I'm not laughing at Los Angeles, honest. Is your name Alan Porter, by any chance? Only I think I might just be the person you've got to meet.'

'Are you Tony Ross?'

As I said yes, we extended hands. His was easy and true.

'Pleased to meet you,' I said. And, what's more, I actually meant it. I didn't tell him that I had expected him to be dripping gold and wearing slacks. Why ruin a good friendship?

Walking into Smith's, though, I thought the choice of restaurant might do just that for me. The décor was ersatz good taste, fake chandeliers and diabolically bad bits of attempted art, ill-displayed on the rag-rolled walls. There was a sculpture that reminded me of an upturned dustbin, and new-age music droning from fake-marble speakers. It didn't seem exactly promising. Nor did the fact that we were left standing awkwardly by some art, while important-looking waiters hovered to no obvious purpose. I finally had to grab one by the arm so that we could be seated.

As a result, we found ourselves squashed behind a pillar, next to the toilets. When I mentioned this to the *maître d'*, he peered down his nose and pointed out that there were only two of us and the other tables were for four, so we could not move. I should have pointed out that his restaurant was half empty and that he was a snotty-nosed wanker who was failing to please two customers. I don't know why I didn't.

Mr Porter, I thought, carried himself with the easy confidence of someone who knows they don't have to prove very much. He also spoke in a soft, rather quiet voice, whose origins I would place somewhere between Wembley and Sudbury. He knew Steiner from many years ago, and respected him, he said, in every sense. He was meeting me for the precise reason that he liked meeting good people, and Mr Steiner had told him I was good people.

I told him that it was my birthday. And in his richly understated manner he told me some things. Such as these:

'There was only one real mod, and he was Lee Daniel's brother.'

'The finest tailor in all of London was called Bob and he had a workshop in Aldgate. He perfected the Biswing back.'

'I once hid a bag of two hundred blues in the foundations of Centre Point when they were building it, and never got them back.'

'The swinging sixties consisted of seven people with a sense of humour and one with a rich dad.'

At this point the menu arrived, written in

incomprehensible *nouvelle* French, and the waiter scoffed when we asked what it all meant. When he had grudgingly told us, Mr Porter continued:

'The greatest fight I ever saw took place in New Orleans.'
'Small things please great minds.'
'Porchester Hall is my favourite place in the world. Terence Stamp goes there.'
'I would have given everything to have made *Spartacus*. It's an object lesson.'
'California is a bit like south London, only hotter.'

Then the beginnings of the food landed on the table. It was pale and it was meagre. But even this did not deter Mr Porter. He smiled with all of his face while he talked, and all the while he talked, I sat enthralled and charmed and entertained. I chipped in my own words at some times, but mostly just sat feeling good in the pleasant presence of a master. We both toyed a little with the meal, for it deserved nothing more. He carried on talking:

'There used to be a club in Kingly Street called the Gestapo, where the governor had a wooden leg. They had tropical fish too.'
'You must remember that in baseball the game is never over until the fat lady sings.'
'Money is a good thing; never let them tell you otherwise. It enables you to follow your curiosity. It's just that sometimes you have to remember to enjoy it.'
'In my opinion Tom Waits's score for *One from the Heart* is the best piece of film music this decade.'

At this point I was presented with a macédoine that looked like a bowl of stewed pears, a small bowl. I instantly backed it, to the shock and chagrin of the waiter, who gave us both leper eyes for my impertinence. I got, I will readily admit, a little wound up, but Mr Porter remained remarkably calm; and, in fact, found the whole thing rather funny. As the very ordinary coffee arrived, he continued telling tales:

'There's a ghost station between Holborn and Tottenham Court Road on the Central Line, called Museum [I told him I knew that one]. I loved the underground as a kid. I was a real tubist; I collected tickets and everything.'

'Joe Frazier is a sweet man.'

'We made *Swinging Up the Jungle*, the first movie for the Tribe, on eighteen grand, and most of that went on Minis. We wrote off loads of them.'

'I like the beach. I just don't like the people who like the beach.'

'I've still got a thing about cinemas, about being there when the darkness ends. I can still be awed and excited and appalled. I cannot lose that, even in Hillingdon.'

'They make the best telephones in Spain.'

Almost everything he said, I considered interesting. And finally, when a cognac or two had fired my chest and given me the courage of a Dutchman, I decided to ask Mr Porter a question. It was something that had been troubling me for some considerable time, and which I thought he might be able to help me with.

'How do you not become bourgeois?' I asked.

I was glad to see that he did not think this was a funny question, but thought seriously for a few seconds and then answered, 'You have, most of all, to remember the things that you really like. Forget that and you are lost. You must also retain your sense of humour and your sense of the absurd. For these are your greatest support in the struggle. Then, finally,' he said, sipping his coffee like a foreigner, 'you must remind yourself every single day of just how much you hate them.' With that he let out a laugh that seemed almost too hearty for his nature.

The bill arrived with all the haughtiness and tardiness

and indifference that had characterized the meal. Mr Porter instantly, but calmly, grabbed it.

'This one is on me, all right?' he said with a serious smile.

'Leave me out. I'm the one playing at home, I get the bill.'

'Please, Tony, I insist.'

I thought, while this little comedy of manners was taking place, how much a part of the expense-account existence this ritual is. It made me feel middle-class just to take part in it, so I gave in quicker than tradition dictates.

'All right, you win, it's on you.'

His smile grew, and I couldn't quite fathom the thinking behind it. He held the bill in his hand as he spoke. 'You sure now, it's on me?'

I felt suddenly embarrassed. Maybe I'd given in too quickly, but I couldn't change my mind now. So I just said yes.

'Good. I'm not going to pay it. The food and the service were shit, and this sort of pretentious place gets right up my nose. Let's do a runner.'

I didn't fall off my chair; I didn't even say, 'You're joking', because I could tell he wasn't. I don't think I said anything, although I may have nodded.

'Right. You go to the toilet now, then after a minute I will leave as invisibly as possible, go and get the car and have it running round the corner. After about three minutes you leave the loo and go straight out of the door. Don't stop, whatever they say. I will leave my business card on the table, so that they can contact me afterwards, and I will tell them why we did it and, if necessary, pay the bill. This will shake them up a little, though. You agree?'

He was rubbing his hands together like a little boy now. I thought of dozens of reasons for saying no. But none of them could overcome the sheer pleasure that he was obviously feeling. So I just held out my hand for another of his pleasing shakes, slipped my jacket on and headed for the toilet. 'See you in four minutes precisely,' I whispered.

When I entered the toilets, it somehow seemed to fit into the scheme of the conspiracy to actually lock myself in a cubicle, even though I had nothing to actually do there. Sitting on the toilet with the cover down, looking at my watch and listening to the sound of people coming in, executing their business and leaving, I thought how funny it is the way things turn out.

Then, after three minutes, I flushed the unused water-closet in order to give a little realism to my performance, left the cubicle, glanced quickly in the mirror and walked purposefully out of the toilet and up the stairs. I had a feeling that everybody was bound to be looking at me, but the few advertising executives and graphic designers still in the place were buried deep in their own domains.

So I strolled as loosely and as quickly as possible across the floor until I got to the door. At that point a waiter gave a cry of 'Sir', but instead of stopping I pushed the door open and half ran, half jumped through it.

I heard a noise behind that was a mix of shouting and movement, but by now I was running left towards the square, driven by a mix of fun and fear. As I ran, I glanced over my shoulder to see a white-shirted waiter running after me. Then suddenly I saw a black-bodied beauty reversing towards me. I ran towards her and, to my horror, she continued to hurtle directly at me at high speed. Thankfully, though, the car stopped with a jolt just as we were about to collide, and I clambered awkwardly over the side, tipping head first into the back seat as we roared off into the sunset.

I poked my head up just in time to see a pair of panting waiters holding theirs in wonderment.

'I think that was fair, don't you?' said my new friend.

We then proceeded to do spring cruising with disco relish round the streets of old and new London. Letting the populace look at his car. I loved it.

For a couple of hours we did this. Visiting such places as the King's Road, Kensington, Hyde Park, the Embankment, the City. And all the while we rode, we talked about the London that we loved and he missed. And I was so deeply and naturally impressed by his enthusiasm that I almost forgot that it was my birthday as I sat and revelled in the glory of this very good car.

But then, just after five o'clock, I remembered that I had to meet my friends at my flat, and so asked Mr Porter if he wouldn't mind taking me home. Of course he did not mind.

Driving back to Wimpole Street, I felt happier about many things.

'Would you like to come up for some coffee?' I said.

'Thank you.'

Walking back into the block, I thought it had been a good day and hoped that Mr Porter would like the décor. We rode the lift to the fourth floor, opened the cage and walked up to my front, brown, wooden door, which I opened with the Yale, and stepped on to the darkly stained floorboards inside.

I turned the corner into the living-room, switching on the light on the way, and there were: Joe and Jimmy Kelly, Gabriel, Little Anthony, Polly Stanford, Margaret, Danny Marney and his wife, Jane, Mr Quick, D J Jay, MacSweeney, Tommy Moore, Fran, the Creature, Squirrel, Bob, the singing girl, Kaitlin, Julie, the Neandersoul Man, Gene Karel.

Afters

Only Rose wasn't there. That's what I thought when Easter came.

She phoned and we spoke and it was good. But it would be nice, I thought, to see her. I've also got to go and see my mum and dad. And I want to see Fulham too. We're playing Brentford, and a win will take us clear of the relegation zone. This would be nice.

I also think I'll take Polly to see my parents. She'd like that. I like her and the freckles on her back. She has never once woken up before me, which is just fine, because it gives me time to think privately and look at her. I don't think I'm in love.

Good Friday is a good day to see your mum and dad when you come from a Catholic family. I see them more now, but today I shall take with me eggs and flowers.

I sat on the bed and kissed her back. Polly always sleeps on her front and sprawls out to compass points. I pulled the duvet back to get a better look. I just wanted to look at her and feel nice. I stroked her a little.

'Do you want coffee?'

She concertinaed her body in and out before turning slowly over to look at me. She looked kindly. 'Um.' She did a bit of blinking and rubbing before settling on her usual slightly dazed smile. Then she unravelled her limbs, stood up and ambled towards the bathroom with her usual aplomb. She shouted up the hall, 'What are we going to do today?'

I followed the sound of her voice and stood in the doorway watching her take a piss. She wiped herself with a tissue with no shame. I walked in and planted a kiss on the top of her head.

'I thought I would introduce you to my people,' I said to a crown of long, red hair.

'What, your mum and dad?' she said, with a pleased tone in her voice. She tipped her head back and peered up with a puzzled happy expression as she put her arms round my waist.

I knew she knew this wasn't a proposal or anything. 'Yes, why not?'

She put on a floral, forties-style dress, which made me smile. Together we bought flowers, lilies and gladioli and roses and tulips, all in white. And we also bought chocolate eggs with various fondants and flavours in a little shop in Marylebone, open for precisely that purpose. We walked around bank-holiday London, and finally hailed a cab.

In the back of a black cab travelling towards old N22, Polly Stanford, with her legs dangling over mine, told me that she had never been able to decide about families. I knew what she meant.

But walking up the garden path to mine, I felt all right. Our house looked as poor as powdered milk and friendly, and the smell of fish that denotes Fridays and high days crept beneath the door, which had never fitted properly. Standing outside it with this girl just felt like an ordinary moment.

My mum answered the door.

She was looking small but quite happy. I hugged her and then I introduced her to Polly. She shook her hand and said the rather formal 'hello' she reserves for young ladies. She beamed at the flowers and blushed at the eggs.

As we moved up the hall, I saw that there was a new plastic strip covering the carpet, which had appeared since I'd last been. I winked to Polly, but said nothing.

My dad was sitting in his chair, watching *Chitty Chitty Bang Bang*. It was the scene where the child-catcher first appears. I've always loved that scene. He smiled at me as he said, 'Hello', and did the same to Polly. He didn't sparkle at her, though. I think in many ways he's given up.

The ornaments were all in place. We ate fish, and my mum said grace, and boiled potatoes and carrots and peas and we sat at the table and talked. We had cans of Coke and Tizer, and a cake that my mum had baked and bread pudding, which I loved as a kid and like as a kid today.

I came from these carpets and these framed photographs and these dusted knick-knacks, acquired over years of having nothing. This isn't me any more, but I long for it to be understood for all its value and its values. I guess mostly I want to understand it myself.

Polly was good. She even suggested that my mum should get the photo albums out, and actually seemed to enjoy it when she proudly pointed out the blurred portraits of the pier at Ramsgate and my Uncle Jack, who used to drink with Johnny Haynes.

My father and I sat and talked for a while about his work, about the government and about football, and quietly about the fact that he was a little worried about Mum. Her circulation is bad and he said he wasn't at all sure that her heart is very strong. I think it was the first time he'd ever said anything like that to me, and I felt oddly touched. He seemed vulnerable.

And while we were sitting in the chairs, me with my hand on Polly's knee and my mum making tea in the kitchen to go with the cake, the telephone, the one that stands on the three-legged corner table, object of much pride, rang. It was Alex.

My brother lives in Balham now, with a girl and a baby I've never met. He was surprised to hear my voice, but I'll give him this, he recognized it straight away.

'Hello, Tony, how are you?'

'I'm good. And you?'

'You know, getting by.'

I was going to go and get Mum when I suddenly thought, why not?

'What are you doing tomorrow, Alex?'

'Nothing. Why?'

'I just wondered if you fancied going to football.'

There was a second's silence.

'Fair enough. Shall we meet in the Orange Tree about 1.30?'

'See you there.'

When Mum had finished on the phone, she went a little quiet. She is still hit hard by what happened to Alex, and with Polly being there, I think she just got a bit embarrassed.

To bring the conversation, and my mother, back on to a happier track, I asked how Maria, Fred, Xavier and their new baby girl were doing. I knew they were doing just fine and I knew my mum would like the chance to say so. The details of the birth were explained in femininely gory detail.

She was in her place, my mother. A place with, I now know, an honour all its own. It took me a long time to see that. But what I come from owes to nobody; it has a sense of fair play and it refuses to feel embarrassed. It is not, as I thought for so long, that they do not want from life, but that they have learned to take pleasure from what is there.

And it was pleasing to see my mum happy. I wanted to touch her and tell her how well she had done, but I couldn't quite. He deserved something good too. I do believe now that he has cared; he just wasn't that well equipped. I can't say that I like him, but I would never now say that I don't.

I had an idea, and it pleased me just to think of it. My mum was preparing sandwiches in the kitchen, standing by the new spin-drier, cutting cucumbers and tomatoes with a

Kitchen Devil and placing them alongside slices of rather sweaty ham in a supermarket bread when I asked her why she didn't go to Spain to see Maria and the kids.

'I'd love to, but we need a new three-piece – this one is going home – and we can't afford both.'

'I'll pay for it.'

She smiled a big involuntary smile before regaining her composure and putting back on her serious face.

'Thanks, love, but you can't do that.'

'Yes, I can. I'll book the tickets on Tuesday. When do you want to go?'

Polly had laughing eyes at the idea. I think she felt good to be part of a happy scene. My mum hugged me and gave me a kiss, the first we've really shared in a long time. I know it wasn't all that big, wasn't exactly history, but it sort of was for us.

That night I slept well and long, in the company once again of my long friend, and thought only of Fulham and football and family. I knew I'd done it for me as much as for them, but that doesn't make it wrong. I will take pleasure from theirs, that's all.

I made Polly toast with the honey she likes and provided the trashy newspaper to which she is addicted. We both drank tea.

The journey across town in a train wasn't really hard. The tangle of tourists and day trippers, shoppers and shop-lifters, girls who work and boys who rarely do was actually entertaining. Everybody seemed to be wearing bright colours and carrying Benetton bags, which is strangely disconcerting when you are off to see Fulham play at Craven Cottage. I saw many people who didn't look like my memories.

I saw nothing, though, of marauding terrace terrors in search of an off. This was a little disappointing, but little else had changed about Saturday, especially the way I felt. I still understood why I got excited. It is nice to know that the thing you thought was so important for all those years really is.

Coming out of the underworld, I laughed.

There were a couple of kiddy casuals, seriously dressed in this season's vogue, slipping small amounts of silver into the hand of the man when I went to hand in my ticket. Those elemental things, of course, never change.

But Fulham has gone. The area around Hammersmith Station remains reassuringly wrecked. But once you escape the flyover, you're into a ghetto. Monotonous, homogeneous rows of hatchbacked houses, where City drones and sons of Sloanes hold barbecues and talk in philistine tones. Gone are the children who scraped their knees and the families who waited in the rain for buses to take them to relatives in Paddington and Shepherd's Bush. Gone even are most of the criminals, to Surrey or somewhere. The river isn't grubby any more; it's lined with estate agents' lights.

I don't know if that old Fulham was worth fighting for. The one where my Uncle Jack, who knew Johnny Haynes, lived until, at the age of thirty-nine, he met my Aunt Ruth at the Hammersmith Palais, got married and moved to Reading. I'm sure that Fulham Football Club must be kept, though, even if the new locals care nothing for the game. Jack still travels in for most matches, and I will not accept that he should be robbed of his culture in the pursuit of developers' profits. Craven Cottage, so full of wonder, cannot be sold so cheaply; it is mine and my history.

I thought all of this, and I thought too that I am going to enjoy being mates with my brother again. Walking to football still makes me think.

Entering the pub, I saw Alex sitting with a pint of lager, reading a copy of the *Sun*. He looked like Alex.

'Do you want another drink, brother?'

'Hello, Tony. Thanks. I'll have a pint of lager.'

We didn't shake hands, we didn't hug or kiss. I didn't hunger like that.

Carrying two drinks across a pub almost crowded with football fans, I felt suddenly uneasy about all this. I hadn't been to see my brother in the year and a half since he'd returned from captivity, and he had made no effort to contact me. Maybe that said something.

'How have you been, Alex?' It seemed like the obvious thing to say.

'I've been all right. It's not exactly easy, but I make ends meet.'

He looked a little fatter than I remembered, but there was the same hurt vacancy in his eyes. The bravado that he once carried with him had gone, though, and he just seemed to me sad. He didn't seem anxious to ask about me – probably didn't want to know – so I continued the questioning.

'Tell me about your wife and kid. What are they like?'

'I'm not married, Tony. The woman I live with is called Janice and she's all right. My daughter is called Jasmine and she's all right too.'

Alex had sounded fine on the phone, but he was undoubtedly giving me grief here. I couldn't work out why, but then I've never been able to understand him. Rather than get wound up, I decided to just let it ride and talk about football instead.

'Have you been coming down here this season?'

'Yes, I've been a bit. I notice you haven't. They've been shit.' There was a badness in his eyes.

'I've been travelling a lot and I haven't really had time.'

'No, I don't suppose you have, Tony. Mum tells me you're doing very well. Mum always tells me you're doing very well.'

Envy is an ugly emotion, especially when worn by my brother. I had come here because he is family, and I thought that family is something I should work at. I also believed that it was now something I could succeed at. But he was just doing his best to remind me that I don't like him. Alex is ignorant and proud of it, the worst kind of small.

'Is there something the matter, Alex? You seem a little upset.'

His face was now full of open contempt. 'Of course there fucking is. Everything's the matter. You come here full of yourself and your life; you're not part of this. You haven't contacted me since I came out of prison, and you wouldn't give a damn if I went back. You don't care for me – you're just trying to make yourself feel good.'

The vehemence and velocity of the attack came as something of a surprise, but the opinions expressed didn't. I talked back.

'What you mean, Alex, is that you're feeling sorry for yourself and you want me to do the same. Well, I won't, because that wouldn't help you. And besides, I just don't feel enough for you for that.'

It was funny. We were arguing with apparent venom, but without aggression or even passion. I had come here hoping to find some blood-rich feelings for the brother I'd lost, and in fact discovered that I didn't really care. It was quite a load off my mind.

'I don't like you, Alex.'

'I don't give a fuck, Tony.'

I went to football alone.

There was good humour there, and I was in good humour too. I sat near Alex the Traveller, a man who had seen every Fulham game, home and away, including pre-season, for the past eighteen years. He reminded me of why I like men. They are capable of such fine romancing.

We lost to the odd goal in three, but were woefully unlucky to do so. We played well and with heart, and indeed there were moments when the young men out there in white shirts and black shorts made me feel ever so proud.

Their rhythms, for the most part, were those of school-boys, but they had all the pride and fight of men in the making. They even, one or two of them, had that special combination of arrogance and ability that makes things possible. Things like taking a football out of the air and sending it in a perfect line for, say, forty yards, and then running to try to do the same thing again without even stopping for praise. Things like nutmegging a man who had played, in his time, for both Arsenal and Aston Villa. Things, I am sure, like winning promotion next year.

I went home not feeling unhappy.

I'd like to go and see Rose tomorrow, I thought. So I spoke to her on the phone and she sounded good, but a little distant. But then, somewhere in Surrey, I guess, is quite a long way.

That night I went to the club. Polly was leaving early next day for New York and wanted an early night's sleep in her own flat. Truth be told, I was glad. Much as I like her, I wasn't in the mood for that girl on that night. I felt like getting drunk in the company of honest men.

Squirrel and Tommy Moore came round to the flat, where we drank a bottle of champagne and talked sport for an hour and a quarter. Then we drove. First into Covent Garden for some bad Mexican food and good frozen Margueritas, cursing the office-workers and born-again trendies drowning this once decent *barrio*.

From there we evacuated by foot to a bar just off St Martin's Lane, which was frequented by a collection of fashion faggots of the type who use such clothes as make them look like fools. It was, though, this week's in place, so we went in. It never does to get too choosy, and I will admit that the place was rocking and rolling in a rather statuesque sort of way. You always get good women, too, where you get bad clothes.

We met Little Anthony there. He was wearing a black

wool-and-cashmere single-breasted three-piece suit and bowler hat, which he had definitely not had made specially for this occasion. Saturday night is rarely an occasion, but I was enjoying myself, enjoying myself with others.

Anthony was back in London for a month and a little fed up with the rigours of being a pop personality in a land where the papers always lie. In the past week it had been reliably reported that he had died of a heroin overdose and married a model he'd never met. Both of these facts upset his mother, who still could not speak English properly, but who had such stories eagerly translated by those who could. I told him what he already knew, that there was little he could do save laugh it off. He is a pop star and he must let icons be icons. All laughed at that line.

The next stop was the Funland amusement arcade in Old Compton Street; Little Anthony cheered up considerably in the presence of such machines. His fluency on the joysticks, the pedals, the steering-wheels and the buttons that wreak such fine vengeance, was lifting just to watch. He strode out of that place a true champion and prepared for the high spirits of the night. I could tell by the way he carried himself.

So we walked among the people and the winos and the Swedes and made our way, in a way we'd done many times before, to the club I think of fondly as home. The Pleasure-dome is almost a monument now.

I still get a thrill from seeing a queue outside our club. It isn't just the money, though I never knock the money. It is seeing it survive, seeing the whole thing grow; it is almost like being told you were right. I also still get a thrill from jumping to the top of queues.

We've got a young boy of the North called Billy working the door Saturdays now. I had a brief chat with him about how business was. Business, it seemed, was just dandy.

In the club in the upstairs bar, in the way that you do, we

met a few friends and said many hellos, and drank beers that got warmer as the night wore on. This was not a radical thing for me. It was, I guess, what I've been doing for ten years now. I like it.

And then a song came on, and it was a song I remembered deep down in the bottom of my feet, that made me dance a serious straight-backed dance, feeling good and happy. And all around me others were doing the same, and that seemed to me a good thing. A good night.

Standing by the bar at the back near the toilets, that night, we reminisced between us about the past and finally promised to do the same tomorrow. Truth be told, tomorrow I'm going to see the girl I love the most.

I cannot say I expected a resurrection, not even at Easter, but you live in a strange half-hope. I don't even know if I really want a reconciliation, but not knowing is just as unsettling. I know I still miss her, and that knowledge is with me all the time. So is the thought that I blew it.

The train ride to Rose was good. That uncluttered, unhurried feeling of travelling when you have no rush and no baggage, save a record wrapped in brown paper. The morning was bright and blue and the British Rail staff polite. And when I got to the small suburban station, Surrey looked very nice. I always thought of this as the kind of place that the rich retire to. Rose has been living there for a year with a man called Graham who drives a fucking BMW and designs the interiors of coaches and camper-vans. I've been to Surrey once before, you may remember. I didn't like it much.

I'd spoken to Rose a lot on the phone; she even calls me sometimes when she's up or down. But we've only met once since we split up; nothing much happened. I didn't know what to feel, and don't know what I felt on that occasion. Today I think I feel all right about it all.

The walk from the station was a short one, and Rose's

directions were just as precise as I expected. It was maybe half past twelve when I walked up to her front door.

Rose opened the door and half hugged me, kissed me on the cheek. She looked pretty much the same. The hallway looked stark and stylish.

'You look well, Tony.'

'So do you.'

It didn't feel like meeting an old friend; it felt like meeting an old lover.

We walked into the kitchen together, I with the record wrapped in brown paper under my arm, she with the upright walk she had always employed. In the centre of the large kitchen stood a heavy, arty table made from, I would guess, bur elm, and behind it stood a boyfriend aged approximately thirty-three. He shook my hand well, if a little nervously, and looked kindly.

'Tony, this is Graham.'

Rose had half a smile on her face, and I got a sense that she was almost enjoying this little scene. He wasn't. I could tell from the way he held himself, the way he said, 'Hello', the way he looked at me close and made it look like he wasn't. He struck me as a good, and probably gentle, person, and I felt a little sorry for him in his embarrassment. I didn't like him, though, so I did nothing to alleviate it. I was pleased to meet him and I wished he wasn't there.

I stood straight and loose in order to hold the higher ground, and smiled my easiest smile. I wanted it to look as though I were enjoying this. But, truth be told, my main feelings were suddenly a mix of melancholy and meanness.

I didn't want to be here in this, to all intents and purposes, happy home. I wanted to be somewhere else and I think I wanted to take her with me. Not necessarily to resume our relationship, just to ruin the one she was now in. I think I had hoped for signs of discord, and instead I'd discovered a cosy sitcom of yuppy loving. I didn't like it.

I didn't like the fact that it all seemed so nice; she'd been to me so much more than nice. And I felt, looking at this soft-suburban kitchen, that I had lost her, the her I knew with all her power and her rightness.

She just said, 'Would you like a drink?'

We had coffees on the arty bur-elm table, coffee made in a chromium machine, and she cracked a joke about how we must start meeting like this. He laughed and ran his hand through her hair, which seemed to me a bit sick. We spoke for a while about little, and Graham apologized to me for the fact that he had to go out to visit his old mum in Staines. How good of him.

Tall, about six two, square featured, with close-cropped hair and pale eyes, he had, I could see, a certain appeal. But there was also a softness about him that I found vaguely revolting. After a few moments' talking, he was gone, and I was glad. The record, still in the brown-paper bag, sat on the table.

With just the two of us in the house, the atmosphere changed, more tense and more close. She showed me round. Stylish and warm, it had her mark. It was also littered with the little things that made up her life, a vase with her favourite peonies, a jewellery box of Chinese lacquer, a horse's skull that I bought her, an African mask. It made me feel part of her, and apart from her. Made me feel lonely.

I gave her the record and she unwrapped it. It was by Eric Dolphy, a man of grave importance and rare beauty. She looked at it fondly as we talked for a few minutes about jazz. I told her that this record contained an especially sad song, and she touched my arm. She didn't play the record.

'Let's go for a walk,' she said. She also said, 'Tony, are you happy?'

We walked along a lane to a park of perfect spring greenness. It was gently beautiful, but I prefer parks when they're in the centre of towns; I like the idea that you're in an enclave. We were walking side by side, not really looking at each other.

'Yes, I think so.' I answered like that because it was true. 'What about you?'

'Yes, very. Things can get a little slow, but he's a good person, Tony, and work is good. I miss you sometimes, but it's for the better.'

'I miss you too, and it hurts sometimes. The worst thing, though, is that I know I was to blame. I only wish I'd been better while we were together.'

Rose turned and looked then, stopping in front of me and looking close. She was smiling, gently, both with her eyes and her body, which made me miss her even more. I wanted to hold her, but of course I didn't.

She spoke in her softest, strongest voice. 'You weren't to blame, Tony. I made you feel bad at the end because I wanted to hurt you, wanted to make you suffer. You weren't bad, you were just growing up, that's all, going through changes. We both were, but I was more in control. I knew where I wanted to go and it wasn't as far as you. I let you get lost. There were lots of times I could have helped you, could have helped us get back, but I chose to let it go.'

I felt bad hearing this, felt like letting the tears come. Here was she being so good about me, taking half the blame, and she didn't even know the half, didn't know about all the others. I felt guilt at her goodness and decided, before a second thought should stop me, to speak.

'Rose, it's good and kind of you to be so nice, but it's more complicated than that. I never told you this, but I was unfaithful. For the last couple of years I was seeing other girls.'

I didn't know what reaction I was going to get. It was part confessional, part test. I know I wanted to see if there was any jealousy left.

She laughed. 'Oh, Tony, you're so sweet. Do you really think I didn't know?'

I made a stuttering noise. She continued, 'And do you still not know that I had just as many affairs as you? No, of course you don't.'

She was still smiling. I was spinning. I didn't know how to react. It certainly hit. I felt like screaming. But I knew how stupid that would be. I just began to cry, just a little.

She didn't reach out and touch me.

'Tony, stop. This isn't a time for sadness. We're honest with each other now and we can really start again. There isn't that much difference between friends and lovers, except friends are more honest with each other. I honestly want you to be a part of my life, and I hope that I can give you something again.'

After that it was all right, not easy, but all right. And I knew, when I brushed aside the self-pity, that we could be good for each other. I knew too that Polly Stanford was nothing more than a mirage. I cannot be dealing with emptiness.

We spoke of other things after that: like my mum and dad, and Pleasure Inc. and England, like movies and interior décor and various gossips. During the gossips she became girl-like and interested, and I remembered that side of her. We ate, too. And I did feel better.

Then her boyfriend came home, and I still didn't like him much. But now I knew that I could grow to enjoy not liking him. I wasn't bitter, but I was a bit battered, and Rose knew.

In the evening I left and, as I did so, Rose saw me to the door, held me sweetly and said, 'Tony, don't allow yourself to be too hurt. Don't expect it all to be too much like a book.'

It was not a long walk to the station. But at moments it felt like it.

The train wasn't late. I don't really believe they often are.

There were some kids in the carriage, maybe six or seven.

They looked full of possibilities and heavy with pleasure. All toy-box clothing and sullen shapes, they were putting on a bright, if a little weary, pantomime of teenage manners that was just a trifle loud for my mood. One of them was boasting a box of sounds, of hip and hop and breaking beats that ricocheted off my nerves and made them dance some. I was feeling a little weary for a Sunday, and at times they were laughing, which made it worse.

I was trying not to think of Rose; there was time yet to let that fall into place. But these kids were giving me a headache, making me feel uneasy and a little angry. And I wasn't sure why.

As we pulled into Waterloo, I picked my way through the jumble of juveniles. I was feeling irritated by their ripped jeans and torn music and thinking about where I would go to dinner tonight when I heard a word that cut me; and that word was Bournemouth.

I wanted to apologize, to say I was sorry, to ask them if they'd had a good time on their Easter beano. I wanted to see where was in, to see what was happening, to tell them that I used to go to Bournemouth every year, to tell them that is where it all began, to tell them, above all, how glad I am it continues. I didn't, of course.

Instead I walked alone through the big station.

I was going to head for a rank and take a cab straight home. But at the last moment I decided to walk a little. I felt attracted by the anonymity of the station and its concrete hinterland. I felt like walking in the Sunday city.

The area around Waterloo is like that around all stations: alive with its emptiness and perfect for a boy with things to think about. Stations let you indulge your loneliness, just like Sundays. And I felt indulgent.

I thought, as I walked out on to the London street, that seeing Rose had made me even more confused. It hadn't exactly made me sad, it hadn't even made me think of what might have been. Instead it made me realize how we take on board the changes.

I skipped across the roundabout. The sky was nearly black and the traffic was rushing with Sunday-evening ease. I thought it all looked very beautiful. Just seeing it lifted my step a little. The finest view of all London comes from the south side, looking home across Waterloo Bridge at night. It's a quiet, sombre carnival of lights that grows in definition and stature as you walk on to the bridge. To the left is the majesty of Westminster, to the right the City. And beneath you runs the river. I know it well, and I know I like it, this most familiar of cities.

I leaned for a little – a little self-consciously, but what's wrong with that? – over the side of the bridge. Looking west, I thought it seemed big and old, and I felt deep-down confused. One side of me felt happy, at home; the other unsure. The scale of it was difficult to accommodate. I looked up at the Savoy and at that clock next door, and it was almost 9.30. I want a drink, I thought.

Turning to face the north, I walked towards the bank, wondering where to drink. My shoulders were loose and I was walking easy. I turned left down the Strand. I was thinking of an old, anonymous, empty pub and wondering where one might be. Then suddenly I stopped as I realized what I hadn't done.

I ran back to the bridge, crossing to the other side with a weave, stopping roughly at the centre, looking east. For a second I caught my breath and inhaled hard to push back the emotions that were gathering round the glands at the side of my throat. Composed now, I said as loud and as straight as I could, 'Paul, we think of you.'

I found a pub in a little side-street near Aldwych Station, and it was close to perfect. All stern and Victorian, green tiled, leaded and frosted and signed, it was a pub. I pushed open the heavy door marked 'Saloon'. The small misshapen, carpeted room contained a pair of courting couples, maybe an American or two and a small huddle of youngish dark-haired men in clothes too dirty even for a working day.

I bought a pint of lager and sat at the table near the lads.

For a while I sat drinking the beer I'd bought, letting all manner of thoughts run round my mind, neither happy nor sad. I watched one of the couples leave, all overaged young love and embarrassingly held hands. I saw an old fellow enter and buy a brandy. I also overheard the muddy men.

They were most parts Irish and most parts happy, these men. Mixing moans and memories and songs, they were milking this drinking time for all they could. They were together and warm, and there was a splendour about them, the glow of which I could feel from two tables away. They were definitely fellows.

Last orders sounded, so I walked to the bar for another pint. This lager was working well, and I had that feeling of wanting more, wanting to drop just a little deeper into the dizzy, hypnotic melancholy of drinking alone. I wanted to sit in this seat for quite some time. Not escaping going home, just enjoying being here. Near these men.

I drank a little more while considering all of this, then realized that I needed to take a piss.

I walked to the toilet. It was tile and porcelain. I stood in front of the white trough, noted the blue crest of the maker, undid my buttons, pulled out my part and began. Just as the flow started, the door swung open and one of the Paddies walked heavily in. He stood next to me and unceremoniously did the business.

'I don't know why we spend all this money just to pour it away in here,' he said in the accent of Meath.

Turning to look at my neighbour, I saw a man in perhaps his early forties with a mess of dark hair and all the angles of an Irishman.

'I wouldn't want to do without it, though,' I said without really thinking.

'No, nor would I, not on a night like tonight anyway.' He was still pissing and he still wasn't looking.

'So you've had a good time, then?' I said.

'Indeed I have.'

'Have you had the crack?' I asked.

He turned round and looked me in the eye and answered, 'The crack. Now there's a thing. The crack, you must understand is all in the looking.'

With that the bell behind the bar sounded, and it struck. I realized that my time was up. My face, I think, looked down.

I turned slowly to leave, my head bowed. Just as I reached for the door I felt a heavy hand tap lightly on my shoulder. When I turned round, the Irishman looked at me and winked.

'Don't look so down, my friend. There's always afters.'

FOR THE BEST IN PAPERBACKS, LOOK FOR THE 🐧

In every corner of the world, on every subject under the sun, Penguin represents quality and variety – the very best in publishing today.

For complete information about books available from Penguin – including Pelicans, Puffins, Peregrines and Penguin Classics – and how to order them, write to us at the appropriate address below. Please note that for copyright reasons the selection of books varies from country to country.

In the United Kingdom: Please write to *Dept E.P., Penguin Books Ltd, Harmondsworth, Middlesex, UB7 0DA*

If you have any difficulty in obtaining a title, please send your order with the correct money, plus ten per cent for postage and packaging, to *PO Box No 11, West Drayton, Middlesex*

In the United States: Please write to *Dept BA, Penguin, 299 Murray Hill Parkway, East Rutherford, New Jersey 07073*

In Canada: Please write to *Penguin Books Canada Ltd, 2801 John Street, Markham, Ontario L3R 1B4*

In Australia: Please write to the *Marketing Department, Penguin Books Australia Ltd, P.O. Box 257, Ringwood, Victoria 3134*

In New Zealand: Please write to the *Marketing Department, Penguin Books (NZ) Ltd, Private Bag, Takapuna, Auckland 9*

In India: Please write to *Penguin Overseas Ltd, 706 Eros Apartments, 56 Nehru Place, New Delhi, 110019*

In Holland: Please write to *Penguin Books Nederland B.V., Postbus 195, NL–1380AD Weesp, Netherlands*

In Germany: Please write to *Penguin Books Ltd, Friedrichstrasse 10–12, D–6000 Frankfurt Main 1, Federal Republic of Germany*

In Spain: Please write to *Longman Penguin España, Calle San Nicolas 15, E–28013 Madrid, Spain*

In France: Please write to *Penguin Books Ltd, 39 Rue de Montmorency, F-75003, Paris, France*

In Japan: Please write to *Longman Penguin Japan Co Ltd, Yamaguchi Building, 2–12–9 Kanda Jimbocho, Chiyoda-Ku, Tokyo 101, Japan*

A CHOICE OF PENGUIN FICTION

Money Martin Amis

Savage, audacious and demonically witty – a story of urban excess. 'Terribly, terminally funny: laughter in the dark, if ever I heard it' – *Guardian*

Lolita Vladimir Nabokov

Shot through with Nabokov's mercurial wit, quicksilver prose and intoxicating sensuality, *Lolita* is one of the world's greatest love stories. 'A great book' – Dorothy Parker

Dinner at the Homesick Restaurant Anne Tyler

Through every family run memories that bind them together – in spite of everything. 'She is a witch. Witty, civilized, curious, with her radar ears and her quill pen dipped on one page in acid and on the next in orange liqueur . . . a wonderful writer' – John Leonard in *The New York Times*

Glitz Elmore Leonard

Underneath the Boardwalk, a lot of insects creep. But the creepiest of all was Teddy. 'After finishing *Glitz*, I went out to the bookstore and bought everything else of Elmore Leonard's I could find' – Stephen King

Trust Mary Flanagan

Charles was a worthy man – a trustworthy man – a thing rare and old-fashioned in Eleanor's experience. 'A vivid, passionate roller-coaster of a book, which is also expertly crafted and beautifully written' – *Punch* 'A rare and sensitive début novel . . . there is something much more powerful than a moral in this novel – there is acute observation. It stands up to scrutiny. It rings true' – *Fiction Magazine*

The Levels Peter Benson

Winner of the Guardian Fiction Prize

Set in the secret landscape of the Somerset Levels, this remarkable first novel is the story of a young boy whose first encounter with love both bruises and enlarges his vision of the world. 'It discovers things about life that we recognise with a gasp' – *The Times*